SHUTTER

SHUTTER

LAURIE FARIA STOLARZ

HYPERION

LOS ANGELES   NEW YORK

First Edition, October 2016
1 3 5 7 9 10 8 6 4 2
FAC-020093-16246

Printed in the United States of America
Set in Sabon
Design by Phil Caminiti

Library of Congress Cataloging-in-Publication for Hardcover
Names: Stolarz, Laurie Faria, author.
Title: Shutter / Laurie Faria Stolarz.
Description: First Hyperion Hardcover edition. | Los Angeles : Hyperion, [2016]
   | Summary: "Day Connor is convinced that a boy she has met is not the murderer the police say he is, but can she prove his innocence—or will the truth change everything?"—Provided by publisher.
Identifiers: LCCN 2015046022 (print) | LCCN 2016002055 (ebook) |
   ISBN 9781484727904 (hardcover : alk. paper) | ISBN 9781484729212
Subjects: | CYAC: Murder—Fiction. | Photography—Fiction. | Love—Fiction.
Classification: LCC PZ7.S8757 Sh 2016 (print) | LCC PZ7.S8757 (ebook) | DDC
   [Fic]—dc23
LC record available at http://lccn.loc.gov/2015046022

Visit www.hyperionteens.com

For Ed, Ryan, Shawn, and Mom,
with love and gratitude

one

I notice him right away, from the moment he steps into the store: tan skin, broad shoulders, and standing at least six feet tall. But it's not just his looks that catch my attention; it's the way he walks, sort of hunched forward, with his eyes focused downward, like maybe he has some secret. He's hiding his face as well. It's partially shrouded by the hood of his sweatshirt. The sides of fabric fold inward, over his cheeks.

The guy—probably around my age, seventeen or eighteen at most—makes furtive glances around the store from behind dark waves of hair that have fallen in front of his eyes.

I look toward the store owner to see if he notices him. He does, and reaches for something beneath the counter. A phone? A baseball bat? Mace? Should I grab Jeannie and bolt?

Instead I take my cell phone out of my pocket, kick it into camera mode, and zoom in, over the shelves, as the guy looks at a display.

I take a snapshot of his profile, but the angle's bad. He won't look up.

"Can I help you?" the store owner asks him.

He doesn't speak, just shakes his head and moves to my aisle. Wearing dark gray pants that get caught beneath the bottom of his shoes, and a tattered zip-up sweatshirt, he's standing only a few feet away now, looking for something specific.

"Are you ready?" Jeannie asks me, moving toward the register with her predictable box of Bugles.

"Just another minute," I tell her.

I've come here on a mission, with a hard-core craving for taffy. The packages of Saltwater Twists are on the shelf above where he's looking. But he's obviously on a mission too, comparing tuna cans like they're diamonds. I mean, does it *really* make that much difference if the tuna's packed in water versus oil? Or if it's albacore rather than chunk-light or yellowfin?

I wish I could freeze the moment—press PAUSE, take another snapshot—but I pocket my phone instead and take a few steps closer. "Excuse me," I say, just inches from him now.

He peeks at me—light brown eyes, a startled expression, a glance toward the mole by my mouth.

I step on the bottom shelf and then reach upward, standing on tiptoes. The box of peanut-butter-flavored taffy is inches from my fingertips. I stretch a little farther, finally able to grab it. But then I lose my footing. My heel drops, and I stumble back.

Off the shelf.

The box of taffy flies from my grip.

The guy stops me from falling by catching me in a backbend of sorts—like one of those ballroom dips they do on dance shows—with his hands around my waist.

I gaze up into his face, noticing a cut on his cheek—a horizontal slash that sits right below his eye. His breath smokes against my forehead. He smells like gasoline and something else. Salad dressing? Garlic oil?

I stand up straight, regaining my footing. "Nothing comes between me and my sugar fix," I say, in an effort to be funny. But it isn't funny and he doesn't laugh—not even a snicker.

The doorbells chime. "What's taking Day?" Tori asks, poking back inside, shouting to Jeannie.

The guy moves to retrieve my box of taffy.

"Thank you," I say, taking the box, telling myself to turn away. But something inside me can't.

Won't.

Because I just have to know: Who is this guy? And what is he hiding from?

"Day?" Jeannie calls out to me.

"Just another second," I holler back. At this point, he must know that I'm stalling because of him. I have my taffy. There's no other reason to linger. "Are you okay?" I ask him, half-stunned to hear the question in the air, out of my mouth.

He hesitates a moment before turning away and exiting the store.

It's time that I leave too. Armed with my box of peanut-butter-flavored math motivation, I pay at the counter and head outside.

Tori and Jeannie are already waiting for me. *"Finally,"* Tori says.

I join them on the bench, placing my hand to my cheek, able to feel the lingering heat.

"Is everything okay?" Jeannie asks.

"Nothing is okay until we figure this out." Tori shoves her phone in my face before I can even get a grip. "What do you think it means?" she asks. "I mean, *'maybe I'll see you around later...'*"

It takes me a beat to figure out that she's referring to a text from Jarrod Koutsalakis, junior class animé artist and her crush-of-the-week.

"Call me crazy," Jeannie says, "but I think it means that

maybe he'll see you around later. Of course, I'm only getting a B in English right now, so my interpretive skills might be lacking."

"Are you kidding?" Tori asks. "This message is reeking of subtext."

"More like it's reeking of dullness," Jeannie says. "I mean, come up with something original already."

"You're missing the point." Tori rolls her eyes. "I mean, like, *why* would he see me around? Like, *where*? Because it's not as if I'll be out on the town someplace special. The highlight of my night includes a pint of Häagen-Dazs and a TV clicker."

"Maybe he's hoping that you *will* be out on the town somewhere," I offer. "Like, at the library or something."

"Does Jarrod Koutsalakis even *know* where the library is?" Jeannie asks. "My vote: he's giving you false hope. I mean, the boy *is* rumored to be seeing Becky Burkus."

"Okay, but Becky Burkus is a total space cadet," Tori snaps, "straight from the Planet Bimbo."

"Right, and you're not," Jeannie says, poking a Bugle into her mouth. "So maybe Jarrod just needs to figure out what he really wants."

Tori drags a strand of her dark pink hair up to her mouth for a nervous nibble. "So where do you think Jarrod likes to hang out? Should I go to the mall tonight? Or maybe to Yoyo's for frozen yogurt...A lot of people like to hang out there...."

I take a deep breath, knowing I'll need at least a few—or twenty—pieces of taffy if I'm going to endure more Jarrod talk. I start to open the package, and that's when I spot him again.

The guy from inside the store.

He's at the opposite side of the parking lot, walking away, down the street.

"Um, hello, is anybody there?" Tori sings, fanning her fingers in front of my eyes.

"I have to go," I tell them.

"Wait, what about Yoyo's?" Tori whines. "Should I go? And, if so, what should I wear? And is it hotter to get the brownie-batter yogurt or the pineapple?"

"Whatever you do, *don't* get the rainbow sprinkles," Jeannie teases. "He'll think you're a ho, for sure."

I get up from the bench.

"No, seriously, what's the rush?" Jeannie asks.

"There's a photo I want to get."

"For real?" Tori sighs. "You're bailing on my crisis for *a photo*? As if the kagillion you have on your hard drive aren't enough..."

I blow Tori a kiss. "I'll call you later. We can discuss the Yoyo crisis then." I turn away and pull my camera out of my bag, my eyes locked on the guy.

two

I follow him for four blocks, keeping a good distance between us. He ends up at the train depot. I take out my phone, pretending to be monopolized by a text, and duck behind a metal post.

I watch him from there. My camera strapped around my neck, I adjust the lens to get a close-up view, able to see a flash of facial scruff on his chin. He moves to the end of the platform where there's a coffee vendor and some newspaper stands. He squats down to read the headlines.

I squat down too and take the shot, cringing at the click of the shutter. Meanwhile, he reaches into the pocket of his pants and feeds the machine a handful of coins.

I take a few more photos.

Click.

Click.

Click.

The noise makes my heart pound, but still he doesn't seem to hear me. He takes a newspaper from the machine and flips it open to the middle to read.

I'm itching to see his hands up close; I wonder what kind of story they'd tell. There's a recycling bin just a few yards away, but if I ran to it, I'd be in complete open view.

The guy crumples the newspaper into a tight ball, kicks the side of the newspaper machine, and throws the ball into the trash, clearly enraged.

A moment later, my cell phone rings: "The Chicken Dance" song. The doors inside my heart slam shut.

I duck back, behind the post, grab my phone, and turn it off.

Holy.

Freaking.

Crap.

Hadn't I turned my ringer off? Did it click back on when I pocketed my phone before?

I venture to peek out again. He's standing now, by the trash can. It doesn't seem he heard my phone either. Or if he did, maybe he simply thinks there's someone waiting for a train, minding his or her own business.

I readjust my lens once more, looking to get an even sharper view. His eyes are fixed on a bag that's sitting at the top of the garbage heap.

He grabs the bag, opens it up, and pulls out what's inside. He turns the thing over in his hand—a half-eaten bagel—as if trying to assess its worth. And then he takes a bite. His eyes press shut. He chews slowly, relishing every bit.

I assume he must be on the run, hiding from someone maybe. His hands are in full view at his mouth; there appears to be something on one of his wrists. I edge out a little farther to take the shot.

My shutter clicks.

His head snaps up.

His eyes meet mine and he stops chewing.

I tuck myself behind the post again. My chest heaves in and out. Blood stirs inside my veins.

But I don't look back. I get up and scurry away, mixing in with other kids on the street, desperate to lose myself in the crowd.

I slipped inside the convenience store, hell-bent on getting food, except there was someone in the aisle that I needed to go down: a girl, around my age. I told myself to be quick. I wouldn't make eye contact. The entire transaction would take twenty seconds, tops.

But then the girl came closer. I could see her inching toward me, could feel her eyeing the side of my face. Was it possible that she knew me? Or did she recognize me from the news?

I gave her some space, assuming that's what she wanted. Meanwhile, intuition told me to leave. But curiosity caused me to look.

I never should've looked.

"Excuse me," she said, reaching for something on the top shelf. She even climbed up on the shelf.

I started to turn away, but then she slipped and I caught her—like a reflex, without even thinking. My hands found the small of her back. My shoulder met her arm. For at least three seconds, her entire weight was supported in my grip.

I haven't touched a girl like that in a long, long time.

Her hair spilled out from the hood of her jacket. She smelled so good—the floral scent of her shampoo tangled with the cinnamon on her breath. She gazed up at me with the palest blue eyes I've ever seen.

I went to pick up the box she'd grabbed. When I gave it back, she said something else—something about sugar. I wasn't really paying attention to her words—too focused on her smile and the giggle in her voice; both of which threw me, because she didn't look scared.

She asked me if I was okay, but I bolted for the door, hating myself for crossing the line. My dad was right. I can be so incredibly stupid at times.

three

It's the following day, and I'm in my room, sorting through images, including some of the snapshots I took at the train depot. I've been thinking about that guy nonstop, wondering if he dropped out of school or ran away from home. *Where does he spend his nights?*

None of my pictures show much of his face, but I do have a nice shot of his hand. I've enlarged it on my computer screen and played with the colors, able to tell there's a tattoo there, on the underside of his wrist, but I have no idea what it's of.

On my way home from school today, I stopped inside that

same convenience store and roamed the aisles, taking my time in choosing, half hoping he might show up. At one point, I could've sworn he was there—could feel someone's eyes watching me from across the parking lot. But when I stopped to look around, I saw that I was alone.

"Day?" my mother calls me.

I get up from my desk and head down the stairs. Mom is standing at the bottom, with her jaw locked in tense mode.

"Is something wrong?" I ask her.

She leads me into the living room, where two officers—a man and a woman—stand by the window, staring in my direction.

"I'm Officer Nolan," the woman says, "and this is Detective Mueller." She nods to the man; he reminds me a little of Mr. Burns from *The Simpsons,* with his bulging eyes and shiny bald head.

Mom places her hand on my back. "The officers are looking for someone, and they were hoping that you could help."

"*Me?*" I feel my face furrow.

"We're searching for a sixteen-year-old male," Officer Nolan says. "He's about six feet tall, with dark hair, olive skin, a medium build—"

Light dawns.

The answer clicks.

My skin starts to itch.

"The suspect escaped from a juvenile detention facility several towns away," Detective Mueller explains. "Someone said they might've seen him in this area."

"He was in the detention center for what?" Mom asks.

Officer Nolan pulls a photo from her pocket and hands it to me. "His name is Julian Roman," she says. "He's wanted for murder."

Wait, *what*? My head spins. My heart tightens.

It's him. The guy from the convenience store—the one from the train depot.

"Does he look at all familiar?" the detective asks.

"I think I remember this case," Mom says. "It happened in Decker, this past spring. Isn't that right?"

My body trembles. Heat rises up, encircling my neck. "I saw him." I nod. "At the food mart."

"*When* did you see him?" Mom nabs the photo from my hand. "And why didn't you say anything?"

"I don't...I mean, I didn't..." I shake my head. The words aren't coming quickly enough. The air in the room doesn't seem ample enough.

"Wait, what's going on?" Mom moves to stand between the officers and me: my very own personal body shield. "How did you know to come here?" she asks them. "And why does this concern my daughter?"

The officers exchange a look. "We actually caught your

daughter on the surveillance video from the food mart," Mueller says. "The owner of the store made a call to the authorities after the suspect left. It appeared that your daughter and the suspect might've had an exchange yesterday. Anything you want to tell us about?" He focuses on me hard.

"He seemed nice," I say, my voice cracking over the words. "He got my candy and caught me when I slipped. But I could tell something wasn't right. I thought that maybe he was hiding from someone, so I asked him if he was okay."

"And what did he say?" Mom asks.

"Nothing." I shake my head. "He left the store without an answer."

"And did you see which way he went?" Officer Nolan asks.

"I did," I say, proceeding to tell them how I had followed the boy to the train depot to take pictures for my project.

"You're kidding, right?" Mom shoots eye daggers at me. She's fully aware of my photography obsession, but said obsession probably doesn't excuse the fact that I shouldn't be stalking strangers (particularly ones that appear so suspect).

"We need to see those photos," Mueller says.

I look back at my mother, gauging her reaction. She gives me a slight nod, and I lead them upstairs to my room. The photo of the guy's hand is still enlarged on my screen.

"I like to take pictures," I try to explain. "To show different perspectives of the same subject . . . It's sort of hard to explain."

But it doesn't seem like they're interested anyway. They're going through my photos, discussing Julian's clothes, his weight loss, and the fact that he was taking a big risk by being out in broad daylight.

"He probably thought he could mix in with the high school foot traffic," the detective says.

"Do you think he's still in this area?" Mom asks.

Officer Nolan looks up from my laptop. Her hair is the color of cranberries. "My guess is no. Most escapees don't tend to stay in one place for very long. They may lay low for a few days, for fear of getting caught on the run, but after that they tend to flee."

"Okay, but *when* did this boy escape?" Mom asks.

"Eight days ago," Officer Nolan says.

"That seems like a long time to *lay low,* wouldn't you say?" Mom folds her arms, back to shooting eye daggers (thankfully not at me this time).

"Well, technically he isn't laying low. The detention center he escaped from is two hours away from here by car."

"Could he be staying with a friend?"

The officer fakes a smile. "Anything's possible."

"And you have *how many* professionals working on this?"

Before the officer can answer, Mom's cell phone rings. She checks the screen and then silences the tone. "Okay, so are we done?" she asks.

"Just about," the officer says.

Mom's phone vibrates again. "Excuse me a moment." She ducks into her bedroom to take the call, desperate to free an American student from a Syrian prison. No joke; my mom is a real-life superhero as founder of Project W, an international nonprofit organization that fights for the rights of women. My dad's not too shabby either as president of the SHINE network, a place that gives second (or third or fourth) chances to those who need one.

I assist the officers by e-mailing my photos to their accounts. They leave shortly after, making me promise to contact them should I see the guy again.

Finally Mom emerges from her room. "What happened?"

I start to tell her about e-mailing the photos, but her phone vibrates yet again. She checks the screen. "I have to take this. Would you mind taking Gigi for a walk?"

Yes, I would. "No, I wouldn't." Still, I grab our neighbor's keys—as well as a bottle of pepper spray (courtesy of Dad)— and head out the back.

four

The leaves crunch beneath my steps as I head down the bike path. Gigi is our neighbor's bulldog. Her owner works as a nurse and often does double shifts, relying on us to make sure that Gigi gets exercise (and bathroom breaks).

It's chilly out, mid-October, and the ground is barely visible with all the fallen leaves. Normally Dad takes care of the yard, but since he and Mom have separated, I'm left to pick up the slack, quite literally.

It's nearing dusk. The smell of a nearby barbecue makes my stomach growl. I continue forward, thinking about the officers' visit, reminding myself that there's still plenty of daylight left, that the guy has probably fled the area, and that there's pepper spray in my pocket.

The wind rakes through the tree limbs, rustling the leaves. Birds twitter. Twigs snap. I tell myself that these sounds are normal and this sudden flutter of anxiety is purely psychosomatic—the result of the officers' probing.

But then I come to a sudden stop, able to hear branches breaking. It's two full breaths before I continue forward again. The roof of Rita's house peeks out over a cherry tree. I go to unlatch her gate, noticing something moving in the distance.

A tree shakes.

Its branches flutter.

There's another snapping sound.

Gigi's barking inside the house.

I pull the gate open. At the same moment I see someone— dark clothes, hunched posture, hooded sweatshirt—about ten yards away.

I tell myself it isn't him. I mean, it can't possibly be him.

My pulse racing, I scoot inside the gate, behind a tree, and pull the pepper spray from my pocket.

But it tumbles from my grip. And drops to the ground.

I look up again, my heart pounding, my head spinning, unsure if he's seen me. He's turned away now, his back toward me, headed for the center of town.

five

I race home—back down the path, across the yard, up the steps, and into the house—locking the door behind me: two bolts, plus the chain.

Mom's holed up in her office, still talking on the phone.

"Mom?" I knock, pushing the door open. It hits the wall with a thwack.

"Yes," she says into the phone, blocking her free ear with a finger.

"This is really important," I persist.

"Could you hold on a moment, Genevieve?" Mom places her

palm over the speaking part of the receiver and finally looks up. "What is it?"

"I really need to talk to you."

"And I really need to free an innocent girl from prison. Can it wait a couple of minutes?"

"Not really."

She holds up her index finger, indicating another minute. "What's that, Genevieve?" She blows me a kiss. "I'll be off in just a bit."

I remain in the doorway for several seconds, listening to her ask questions about the accused girl's whereabouts at the time of her supposed crime.

Finally, I go up to my room, grab my laptop, and open it on my bed. A quick Google search with the words "Julian Roman," "Decker, MA," "Fairmont County," and "Roman murder" and several news stories pop up.

JUVENILE SUSPECT MISSING FROM DETENTION CENTER

WEBER, MA—A male, 16, was reported missing from the Fairmount County Juvenile Detention Facility. The suspect, Julian Roman of Decker, had last been seen in the center's courtyard at approximately 4 p.m. on Tuesday, October 6th.

An officer at the center reported Roman missing at 6:45 p.m. when he failed to show up for dinner. Roman, described by officers as quiet, keeping to himself and often writing in his journal, had been awaiting trial for the alleged murder of his father. Roman is reported to have dark hair, brown eyes, an athletic build, and to be six feet tall. He has a tattoo of a pickax on his wrist, and was last seen wearing an orange suit from the detention center. Anyone fitting his description should immediately be reported to the Weber Police Department.

BODIES FOUND—FOUL PLAY SUSPECTED

DECKER, MA—The body of a forty-five-year-old man, Michael Roman, was discovered at the family home in Decker Village Park at approximately 7 p.m. on Saturday, May 4th. Police were called to the scene. Investigators say the victim suffered head injuries.

The body of a forty-two-year-old woman, Jennifer Roman, was also discovered at the time of the investigation. Ms. Roman's body was found in the bathtub with the water still running. The cause of death is unconfirmed at this time.

The investigation is ongoing as officials wait for autopsy results.

INVESTIGATION CONTINUES IN DECKER VILLAGE HOMICIDE CASE

DECKER, MA—Autopsy results conclude that Michael Roman, 45, had been struck on the head with a blunt object on the afternoon of May 4th in his Decker Village Park home. The murder weapon has yet to be discovered. Mr. Roman was reportedly seen in front of the family home just prior to the estimated time of his death.

Autopsy results also conclude that Jennifer Roman, 42, died from asphyxia due to drowning. Roman's body was discovered in the family's bathtub. Results conclude that Roman had been under the influence of prescription medication, which may have contributed to her death. It's unclear at this time whether she died before or after her husband.

Chief Investigator Pat Chalmers states, "There are no clear-cut answers in this case. However, we're working hard to map out exactly what transpired during the last eight hours of this couple's life." If anyone has information pertaining to this investigation, please contact Investigator Pat Chalmers at the Decker Police Department.

TEEN ARRESTED FOR HOMICIDE

DECKER, MA—A 16-year-old juvenile male has been charged with the murder of his father, Michael Roman, 45, of Decker Village Park, three months after Roman's body was discovered in the family home on May 4th, having been struck with an unidentified blunt object. Michael Roman's son's arrest follows an intensive investigation.

A fellow student of the teen suspect states, "Julian always talked about hating his father and wanting him dead. It was actually pretty scary."

Another student adds: "Julian used to talk about *getting rid of his dad*. I wish I'd said something sooner. I just never thought he was serious."

Jennifer Roman's body was also discovered in the family home on May 4th. Mrs. Roman, 42, had reportedly died from drowning after taking an excess of prescription medication.

The teen suspect will stay at the Fairmount County Juvenile Detention Facility as he awaits trial.

An online comment in response to the last news article states: *"This has got to be the most blatant corruption of justice I've seen to date. No murder weapon? Three months to make an arrest? And what seems obvious to be a murder-suicide situation? You say there are no clear-cut answers, but all you have for us taxpayers are incoherent quotes from a bunch of idiotic kids? Where are the facts of this case? Clearly this is yet another example of Weber and Decker police investigating at its finest. Why am I not surprised?"*

I close my laptop and go back downstairs. Mom is still on the phone. I peek my head into her office, but she's shouting now, into the receiver—something about due process and exculpatory evidence.

In the kitchen, I feed my confusion with leftover chow mein, straight out of the carton, while Officer Nolan's business card stares up at me from the table. Maybe I shouldn't wait for my mom to make the call.

But what if the guy I saw on the bike trail wasn't Julian Roman after all? Or what if the person who commented on the news article has a point about Julian's case being mismanaged?

Is that really my concern? Should I even care?

I reach the bottom of the Chinese food container, wishing there was an extra egg roll—or something—because I have way more questions in my head than Fung Wong's has takeout.

So I followed that girl from the train station, hoping I might be able to snatch her bag and take her camera. She obviously recognized me from the news—was probably planning to share her photos with the police. Part of me was also curious about her—about who she was, and why she bothered to take pictures rather than calling the police on the spot. I mean, she totally could've gotten my ass bagged.

I used to follow my dad too. My brother Steven and I both did. We'd hide in the bushes when he was out mowing the lawn, and then sneak after him when he'd go down the street for beer and cigarettes, ducking behind parked cars every few yards so he wouldn't catch us spying.

Dad was my hero then, back when Steven and I were five. I used to try to do everything the same as him: finger-whistle, throw a Frisbee, slick back my hair, snap my fingers. Crazy to think that it was just a few years after that when I started fantasizing about his death.

six

I wake up late the following morning.

My alarm. Never. Went off.

I fly out of bed and pull on some clothes. "Mom?" I call, figuring she must be in her office. But her office is empty, and so is the kitchen.

I find a note on the table.

Good morning, Day!

I'm so sorry we didn't get a chance to talk last night. Sorry I'm missing you this morning as well. I had to run out for an early meeting at the state house, but I promise

we'll talk tonight. Be sure to lock up, and have a great day!
Good luck with your meeting.

Love,

Mom

xoxo

Beneath the notepad, there's a box of powdered doughnuts (so much for all her preaching about eating only wholesome, unprocessed foods).

I scurry up the stairs, two steps at a time, able to hear a clamoring sound outside. I rush to the window, but I don't see anything. Clearly I need to get a grip. But I didn't sleep well. Plus, I have a French quiz today, not to mention the first meeting of Peace, Brains & Justice (PB&J for short), of which I'm the founding president. I've been planning the meeting for weeks, preparing what I will say and making posters to entice people to come, trying to heed my parents' advice about putting my own personal stamp on the world.

With only ten minutes left before I'm supposed to leave for school, I pull my hair into a ponytail, hurry the cookies I made for the meeting into a container, and grab all my school stuff.

I head out the back door, catching a reflection of myself in the entryway mirror: no makeup, pasty-white face. There's a knot in my hair and a grease stain on the front of my sweatshirt, right over my left nipple.

So. Not. Presidential-worthy.

I close the door behind me, accidentally dropping the container of cookies. Luckily the cover remains intact, but I'm not brave enough to check the aftermath within.

It's still somewhat dark out. The moon sits in the center of a bright violet sky. I approach the bike path, able to feel anxiety stirring up inside me like a hot, bubbling cauldron.

A rustling noise startles me—like a shifting through the fallen leaves. I look all around—toward the back porch, at the windows of our barn, and around the perimeter of the yard—suddenly feeling like I'm being watched. But I don't see anyone lurking.

Still, I take the main road in front of the house, knowing this route will add at least seven minutes to my trek but that it's also the least likely to render me tied up in the back of a van en route to the nearest sinkhole. I haul ass the entire way, booting it for twelve blocks, hiking up the sledding hill, and cutting through the center of town.

Finally I make it to school, but I'm six minutes late and awarded with a big fat detention.

"Please," I beg the school secretary. "Can't detention wait until tomorrow? I have a meeting after school."

"Should've thought about that beforehand," she sings. There's an evil smile across her spray-tanned face.

"Okay, but I've never been late before—like *ever*...in my more than two years here."

"Sorry," she says, still smiling. "See you at two thirty in the Detention Dungeon."

Maybe a dungeon is where I belong, because I look like hell. And now I'll be late for my meeting. Plus, my cookies are all crumbled.

But I almost don't even care.

I'm just happy to not be alone.

seven
seven

I try my best to concentrate in classes, but between my lack of sleep, my train wreck of a morning, the PB&J launch meeting, and the fact that I'll now be late for said meeting because I've been blessed with detention, I'm lucky to spell my Frenchified name correctly (*Jour,* for the record; the French word for *day*), never mind convert *le plus-que-parfait* to *le futur antérieur.*

"How did you do on the French quiz?" Jeannie asks, peeking at me over the rims of her tortoiseshell eyeglasses. The frames go nicely with her new haircut—a chin-length, purposely lopsided dark chocolate bob that makes her blue eyes pop. "Because I totally bombed the bonus."

She, Tori, and I are sitting in our usual spot in the cafeteria—close enough to the exit doors that we can make a quick escape, but far enough from the kitchen that we don't have to endure all the funky fumes.

"There was a bonus?" My stomach twists.

"*Two* bonuses, actually. Baudelaire questions... on the board. Didn't you notice? Madame E announced it."

I shake my head, with a sudden loss of appetite—and the cafeteria's gelatinous fish chowder doesn't help.

"Too busy thinking about your PB&J meeting today, am I right?" Her emerald-studded eyebrow shoots upward, accusingly. "This do-gooder organization is totally going to be the GPA-point-shrinker for you, isn't it?"

"It's supposed to be the college-application-booster, actually."

"Don't get me wrong," she says. "I'm sure it'll be huge. I mean, right?"

"A meeting about sandwich condiments?" Tori snickers. "Where's the sheet? Sign me up."

"Exactly." Jeannie smirks. "I mean, how could it fail? Plus, you *did* promise store-bought cookies, right?"

"And cookies go *great* with PB&J." Tori winks, her eyelids lined with thick black cat's-eye wings. Her style du jour is inspired by some rockabilly girl group from the '50s (or so she says): short-sleeved blouse, waist-cinching belt, pencil skirt, and red leather pumps that match her lipstick.

"For your information, the cookies are *homemade*," I tell them. "Plus, this meeting has nothing to do with food, and everything to do with social justice and human rights—with making the world a better place."

"One sandwich at a time." Tori wipes an invisible tear from her cheek.

"Ha-ha," I drone, flicking a carrot disk in her direction. It lands in her Wilma Flintstone hair (tunnel of bangs, length pulled back in a bun). "Sorry." I suck in a laugh.

Tori's laughing too. She takes a fork to her hairspray-shellacked bangs and tries to stab the carrot out.

"Public forking...real classy," Jeannie says.

"Ugh," I groan. "The meeting today is going to flop." I cover my face with my hands, accidentally plunking my elbow into the pool of ketchup—as if this day couldn't get any messier.

"Because of your wardrobe selection?" Tori frowns at my grease-stained sweatshirt.

"More like because I didn't get any sleep. Any chance the police came to either of your houses last night?"

"If only." Tori gives her yogurt spoon a serious lick. "I could've used me a little hunky-officer-jumping-out-of-a-cake and/or-singing-me-a-telegram excitement."

"I think you can take that as a no," Jeannie says to me.

"Well, they came to *my* house," I tell them.

"And we're just hearing about it *now*?" Jeannie asks.

"Apparently, when we all went to the food mart after school the other day, the police caught us—or at least me—on the surveillance video at the same time that some guy who'd escaped from juvie was in there."

"And so the police came to your house, *because* . . . ?" Tori asks.

"Because I talked to him—the escapee, that is. The police wanted to know if he said anything significant."

"And did he?" Jeannie asks.

I shake my head.

"Wait, was this the hot homeless guy?" Tori asks. "Because I totally remember: He was wearing a hooded sweatshirt."

"Okay, why can't I recall even a smidgen of this?" Jeannie asks.

"Apparently Hot Homeless Guy was arrested for killing his father," I explain. "He was being held in a juvenile detention center before he escaped."

"Okay, I think I vaguely remember this story," Jeannie says. "Didn't it happen last winter?"

"This past spring, actually."

"And now the guy's lurking around in convenience stores?" Jeannie asks.

"Not to mention on the bike trail behind my house."

"Seriously?" Jeannie gawks at me.

I look at the clock: only two minutes left before the bell rings. "Okay, the meeting," I say, completely switching gears. I slide the agenda in front of her.

"Whoa, wait, are you kidding me?" Jeannie balks. "An alleged murderer hanging out on your bike path, not long after conveniently bumping into you in a food mart, is way more important than some dumb meeting."

"*Dumb?*"

"Not dumb." She grimaces. "Just..."

"Curious," Tori says, stealing the conversation. "I am, that is...curious about your club's acronym. What does the *B* in PB&J stand for? Boys? Babes?"

"Try *brains*." I give her a pointed look.

"And what, pray tell, do brains have to do with peace or justice?"

I roll my eyes, as if the answer's completely obvious. It isn't. I know that. But it's too late to turn back now. "Okay, fine. The idea was stupid, but I thought PB&J had a catchier ring than just P&J."

"Like a pajama party." She laughs. "At least we know of one peace-loving soul who's sure to show up to get his PB & Jam on."

She's talking about Max Terbador—no joke, that's his real name; his parents are obviously cruel. Max has been crushing on me since freshman year—since I linked my arm through his in the parking lot after a football game, pretending that we were a pair, thus saving him from Tommy Hurst and his posse of lemmings. They'd been bullying Max for months—for no other reason than the fact that they were assholes (of course, Max's name probably didn't help).

Max was eternally grateful, especially because Tommy had been crushing on me at the time. And so not only had I foiled Tommy's plan to de-pants Max in the parking lot that day, thus crowning him Max-terbater of the year, but I'd also publicly displayed my choice by resting my head on Max's shoulder.

"Max and I are just friends," I remind her.

"One appropriately timed exchange of tongue spit can change all that, don't you think?"

"I'm not even going to dignify that question with an answer."

"Being dignified is way overrated," she says, back to forking at her bangs. "What I wouldn't give for Jarrod Koutsalakis to get all PB & Jammy for me."

"Okay, um, *ew*." I make a face.

"Max is really sweet," Jeannie says, looking in his direction, four tables over.

He's sitting with the hipsters today. Somewhat of a social floater, he tends to gravitate from group to group, not really clicking with anyone in particular.

"Do I smell a crush?" Tori asks her.

"What you smell is your cheap hair spray." She reaches across the table to pluck the carrot from Tori's bangs, once and for all.

Meanwhile, Max looks up in our direction. He stops talking. His face brightens. A smile crosses his lips. His hipster friends turn to look at us too, pausing from their coconut water and bento boxes. Max waves in our direction.

"That boy is way too cute to be single," Tori purrs. "One of you *has* to go say hello."

But before Jeannie or I can even consider the option, the bell rings and we're saved. I give Jeannie the folder for the meeting, also reminding her not to forget about my cookie crumbles. Or maybe that would be preferable.

eight

By the time I get to the classroom for my PB&J meeting, I'm all out of breath, and almost out of hope. It seems the only one who bothered to show up—aside from Jeannie and Tori—is Max.

"Holy freaking flop," I say, thinking about all of the announcements I'd made and the posters I'd put up.

"It wasn't a *total* flop." Tori nods to the empty container of cookies. "Your chocolate-chip crumbles were a hit. A bunch of the science league members grabbed a handful on their way out to hunt for crickets."

"As if that's supposed to make me feel better."

"There was a lot going on today," Jeannie says, trying to apply a verbal Band-Aid. "There were theater tryouts...."

"Plus a marshmallow-eating contest at Bubba Joe's Café," Tori adds. "The winner gets free hot cocoa for a month."

"Well, how can I compete with that?"

"But *we're* here," Jeannie cheers.

"Despite the fact that we really love marshmallows," Tori continues. "Especially tall, dark, and handsome ones." She nods to Max.

While I've been busy squawking, he's been busy cleaning everything up, collecting the handouts and sweeping the cookie crumbles. Tori moves to stand behind him, turning her back to Jeannie and me to do that thing where you wrap your arms around your shoulders and tilt your head from side to side, making it look like you're hard-core kissing.

"Max, you really don't have to do all that," I tell him.

"I don't mind." He turns to face us.

So cute, Tori mouths at me, followed by an exaggerated wink.

"So, are we ready to start the meeting?" Max slides a bunch of chairs into a circle and takes a seat in one of them. "Shall we wage the war on hunger? Create awareness of child labor? Or support prisoners of conscience, maybe?"

"And speaking of prisoners..." Jeannie folds her arms and glares at me. "Shall we discuss the *escaping* variety?"

"Like the ones who off their fathers, break out of juvenile detention centers, and then stalk our good friends?" Tori asks.

"Precisely the variety I was thinking of." Jeannie gives her a high five.

"I'm not sure I know that kind," Max says.

Jeannie, Tori, and I join Max in the circle, and then I spend the next several minutes catching them all up on the convenience store encounter, the photo shoot afterward, and the visit from the officers last night.

"If he saw you taking his picture, he's probably lurking around to get his revenge," Jeannie says.

Max shakes his head. "I think this guy has way bigger problems than some girl who took his picture."

"Sounds like you're taking for granted that he's of sane and sound mind, rather than a deranged serial killer looking to flambé one of our best friends," Jeannie says.

"Deranged serial killers don't go to juvie," Max tells her.

"Do you speak from experience?"

He gives her a freakish look, complete with buggy eyes and a flash of teeth. "What do *you* think?"

I pull my laptop out of my bag and read aloud a couple of the news articles I found.

Tori raises her hand, as if we're in class. "Why do you have creepy articles saved in your Favorites folder?"

"Because I was curious about him." I shrug. "About the

case, that is. I mean, look at things from my perspective: I bump into some guy while shopping for candy. The next thing I know, he's an alleged murderer, on the run, lurking around not far from my house."

"And are you *still* curious about him?" Jeannie gives me an accusatory look, with her eyebrow raised high.

"Maybe I'm not quite convinced he's guilty."

"Because hot guys don't kill?" Tori smirks.

"What if we made this case our mission?" I ask.

"You're kidding, right?" Jeannie glares at me over the rims of her glasses.

Meanwhile, Max has already done a search on Julian's name. He scrolls through the headings on his phone. "Okay, admittedly the case *does* sound a little weak—at least just from these articles."

"But they must have hard evidence," Jennie says. "I mean, they don't just go arresting people without it."

"So how come the articles don't mention the hard evidence?" I ask.

Tori takes my laptop to read one of my "favorite" news reports. "How come Julian's not being blamed for his mom's death too?"

"Because it sounds like his mom committed suicide," Max says.

"But what if she didn't?" Tori taps her chin in thought.

"What if her body was just made to look like she did? Or what if she *did* commit suicide, but only after killing her husband?"

"Then Julian would be innocent," Max says.

"Think about it," I say. "We have a suicide. And we have murder. The two go together like..."

"PB&J?" Tori laughs.

"Don't you want to research this more?" I ask, completely stoked at the opportunity. "To find out if there's a chance he might really be innocent?"

"Okay, in theory, it might be fun," Jeannie says.

"But in reality, I have, like, a bajillion trig problems to do." Tori loops an invisible noose around her neck and pulls.

"Meeting adjourned." Jeannie stomps the heel of her shiny black Mary Jane—her makeshift gavel—against the laminate tile, totally bursting my proverbial bubble.

nine

After the meeting, Tori nabs Jeannie, purposely—and obnoxiously—leaving me alone with Max.

"Thanks for coming to the meeting," I tell him.

"Are you kidding? I wouldn't have missed it." He smiles.

I smile back, but it isn't with the same emotion. Part of me wishes that it were—that I felt the same way about him. But to me he'll always be the boy who on the first day of kindergarten dressed up as Aquaman and peed on the slide, claiming it was anti-villain venom.

"Can I give you a ride home?" he asks.

My gut reaction is to tell him no. But since Tori and Jeannie have already left—and since I'm still feeling a bit creeped out about our resident detention-center escapee, I nod and say yes.

He takes my backpack, ever the gentleman, and we walk out to his car. On the drive to my house, I fill the awkward silence with small talk about things we pass along the way: the Pretzelria, the Taco Teepee, and my newly hated establishment, Bubba Joe's Café. Finally, after several painful minutes, we pull up in front of my house. The inside is dark. My mom isn't home yet.

"Thanks for the ride," I tell him. "Sorry the meeting was a bust."

"It wasn't a total bust. Three people showed up."

"Three of my closest friends."

"Do you really consider me a close friend?"

"Of course I do," I say, stretching the truth like rubber. In theory: I'd love to spend more time with Max. In fact: I don't want to give him the wrong idea.

I thank him again and grab the door handle to exit his car.

"Hold on," he says. "I'll walk you in. Rumor has it there are criminals lurking about." He takes my bag and follows me up the walkway, accidentally stepping into a hole in the ground. He stumbles forward, catching himself on one knee.

"Are you okay?" I blurt.

He gets up. The knee of his jeans is covered in mud. "Groundhog problem?"

"Gardening problem." I grimace. "Believe it or not, that was my dad's attempt at trying to plant a tree."

"Is he aware that one needs to refill the hole once the seed is planted?"

A banging noise startles me. It came from the side of the house, behind the fence. I peer in that direction, wondering if a squirrel might be picking at the trash or scampering in the gutter.

"*Day?*" Max asks.

"Want to come in for a minute?"

"Sure." He perks up.

I lead him up the front steps, and we go inside.

"You know, for as long as we've known each other, I've never been in your house," he says.

"Well, you haven't exactly missed much." I lock the door behind us and flick on some lights so he can get a better view. Only half of the stairwell is painted. The floors are bare and splintery, and our furniture—what we found at yard sales, mostly—is sparse and retro (and not in a funky, eclectic sort of way). It's not that my parents are lacking funds; what they're lacking is time and interest. "Can I get you a washcloth for your pants? And maybe something to drink?"

"A drink would be great."

We go into the kitchen. Max takes a seat at the island, and I open the fridge. There's a half-gallon of milk (expiration date:

four days ago), a bottle of tomato juice, and one of my mom's green drinks (which has now turned brown). "Water?"

"Perfect."

I set our drinks down on the counter and take a seat beside him, still wondering about the noise at the side of the house.

"So, what do you think about starting your club with just the four of us?" Max asks. "I'm sure more people will eventually join."

"Honestly?" I sigh. "I don't know what to think."

Max takes a sip from his glass (a recycled relish jar) and makes a face, startled by the ridges on the rim.

"Sorry." I swallow down a giggle. "My parents are wannabe recyclers."

"Wannabe?"

"Meaning that most of our recycle bins have turned into storage containers." I nod to the bins full of cat food in the corner.

Max swivels to look, and I take a mental picture of him. Gone are the iron-creased pants and shiny leather loafers, replaced with dark-washed jeans and suede ankle boots. His hair has changed too—no longer cut into a bowl, but waved to the side with a sharp razor edge. He looks so different than just two years ago. So, where have I been? Why hadn't I noticed?

He swivels to face me again, totally catching me spying. "Well, I could help if you want." He bites back a grin. "With the marketing, that is. We could put flyers on everybody's windshields and come up with a clever catchphrase to nab people's attention."

I can hear the excitement in his voice. I wish I could bottle it up and drink it down. This meeting—the PB&J organization—was supposed to make me feel that way...give me a sense of purpose. But right now, the only thing that sounds exciting to me is delving into Julian Roman's case.

"It didn't seem as if anyone liked my idea for a first mission," I venture.

"The father-killer from juvie. Were you actually serious about that?"

"Why not? Someone's freedom may be in jeopardy."

"Okay, but you don't even know this guy."

"I know that I have questions. I mean, what if he's really innocent?"

"If he's really innocent, then he should go to trial and be exonerated. Why be on the run at all?"

"Good question."

"You're not planning to go all *CSI* on me, are you?"

"*CSI*? No. But Chelsea Connor, maybe."

"Chelsea Connor?" His face scrunches up with confusion.

"My mother. She's a legal superhero, remember?"

"Oh, right." He nods, still every bit as confused.

"More water?" I stand up from the island, purposely looking

out the window. One of the larger tree branches—behind the barn, at the beginning of the bike path—has fallen onto the ground.

"Everything okay?" Max asks.

"Broken tree limb."

He stands beside me to look. "How far down the bike path did you see that guy?"

"About a five-minute walk."

"I'm sure it's a coincidence, but just in case"—he reaches into his pocket and hands me his cell phone—"you should probably give the police a call."

I nod and start to dial.

I was standing at the side of the house when I heard a loud bang. It was followed by another bang. I peered out through the gate. There was a dark green Wrangler in the driveway.

Day was there. Some guy with her. They were just getting out of his car, and he was totally scoping her out—so much so that he tripped. He stepped into a hole, nearly falling flat on his face. Day reached out to steady him, and his whole body stiffened. If they're seeing each other, it's the start of a new relationship, because she definitely makes him nervous.

My mother used to get nervous too—all the time, when I was younger. "Can I get you anything?" she'd ask my dad. "More steak? Another drink? Are the potatoes warm enough?" She'd pace back and forth in the kitchen, itching her palm, watching him eat, nibbling her nails down to the quick—until the nubs of her fingers were raw and bleeding.

It wasn't until Dad was done with his food that I was

allowed to eat. Mom never ate. Instead, she'd go into the room I'd shared with Steven. I'd watch her from the kitchen table. She'd sit by his bed and read aloud from one of his books, as if Steven was tucked in beside her.

She'd never done that with me.

"Want to come in for a minute?" Day asked that guy.

The cool autumn air swept over my shoulders, giving me a chill. I looked down into the trash can. I'd wanted to pack up more food, but I suddenly felt sick.

While Day and her boyfriend headed for the front of the house, I yacked up the contents of my stomach, able to hear my mother's voice inside my head reading Steven a bedtime story.

ten

The police arrive about thirty minutes after I call them. Max stays until they get here, promising to call me later, after his shift at the boat shop (for which he's already late).

While I stay inside the house, the police search the bike path. It isn't until forty minutes later that Detective Mueller finally emerges from the woods. Officer Nolan follows.

I unlock the door to let them back in. "Did you find anything?" I ask them.

"Looks like someone might've been trying to make a path through the woods," the detective says. "There was an area about thirty yards down where the bushes got trampled and some of the tree limbs were broken, but it only stretched about ten feet."

"Our guess is that whoever did it either found another way or simply changed his mind," Nolan says. "Otherwise, it all looked pretty clear, but we'll have some officers patrolling the area, just in case."

"In case he comes back?"

"If it even was him," she says. "You didn't see his face, correct?"

"No." I shake my head.

"And, as you probably well know, these woods are pretty popular at night. We found beer cans, cigarette butts, and lots of empty bottles. Seems we may need to have some of our officers on party patrol."

It's true. My parents are always complaining about the kids who abuse these woods. They've called the police on more than one occasion, and have gone out themselves to break things up.

"We recently received two calls from the town of Millis," Detective Mueller adds. "It seems that someone fitting the suspect's description was seen early this morning digging inside a Dumpster and then breaking into a parked car."

"Millis?" I ask, trying to picture where it's located.

"The train by the high school goes to Millis," the detective says. "It's about three hours north."

Three hours away.

The tension in my heart lifts.

Officer Nolan hands me another business card. "But please, call us for anything—even if you think it's nothing."

"Thank you," I say, watching them leave—out the back door and around to the side yard—trampling through the six inches of leaves that I still have to rake.

"Serves you right"—Dad's voice was inside my head. *"What were you even thinking? Steven would never have been so stupid."*

I woke up. My clothes were soaked. My hair felt wet. I was burning-hot, and shivering from my sweat. I tried to get up, but the motion made me sick. The sound of my retching filled the dark silence, but I couldn't help it. My stomach convulsed. My nostrils filled with acid as I heaved over and over.

My mother continued to read from Steven's storybook. Her voice played over my father's words: "But Detective Panda had another idea in mind: he was going to help save the town of Panderville by finding that pesky sock thief."

My head ached. The room wouldn't stop spinning. I covered my ears, trying to muffle their voices.

"You have to dig a whole lot deeper than that," Mom said.

"Keep going until the soil changes color. That's when you know you've gone deep enough."

"It's because of you that your brother's gone," Dad told me.

Their words were haunting me. My body was punishing me.

The door flew open then. Footsteps moved in my direction. The toolboxes opened and closed behind me with a clank. I closed my eyes, huddled against the wall with a tarp pulled over me like a blanket.

Was that the mower being moved? The blower being jostled? My water bottle being kicked?

There was more shifting against the floor. Someone was getting closer, just to my right and then over to my left. Where had I left my backpack?

I sucked in my breath. Droplets of sweat dripped down my face. My throat burned.

Things went silent for a moment—all except for my heart. It pounded in my chest; the sound echoed inside my brain. I clenched my teeth, half-tempted to come clean. Were they watching me shivering my ass off? Was the tarp jangling along with my nerves?

I lay there, frozen, trying not to breathe, feeling like I was going to yack again. There were voices outside. They mixed with the words in my head.

Finally, the person moved away. The door closed with a thwack. I got up to bolt.

eleven
eleven

I open the door to the barn. The air inside smells damp, like rotten wood. There's a row of tools hanging on the wall. I go to reach for the rake, wondering where the leaf bags are. I search around, suddenly noticing that the space looks off. The snow blower and lawn mower have both been moved. Dad's toolboxes are all lined up in a row. The sandbags are no longer collected in the corner.

There's a tarp stretched out on the floor—the same one Dad uses for camping trips. I go to pick it up.

And that's when I see him.

His face is only partially obscured by the tarp.

My heart tightens. The room starts to whir.

"Day?" Mom calls.

I peer over my shoulder. The door to the barn has fallen partially closed.

"Are you out here?" Mom shouts.

I exit the barn, feeling like I've just been shot out of a cannon: dazed, confused, shocked, out of sorts. Did that really just happen? Did I really just see him?

Mom's standing on the porch. There's a smile on her face— the first one I've seen on her in weeks. It fades when she sees me. "Is everything okay?"

I cross the yard. My head feels woozy.

Mom places her hands on my shoulders and looks straight into my eyes. "What's wrong?" she asks.

If I tell her the truth, the police will come. Is that what I want?

My body trembles from the cold. I need time to process everything. "I'm feeling a little dizzy," I tell her. It's the truth, after all.

"Come inside," she says, taking my hand.

I turn to look over my shoulder at the barn, wondering if he knows I saw him.

Mom leads me up to my room and tucks me beneath the covers. "I'll fix you some tea and toast. Then we can talk, sound good?"

It does. I nod and then turn over in bed. I pretend to fall asleep so I don't have to talk. But the truth is that I don't sleep all night. I just stare toward the window, hoping he'll be gone by morning.

I tried to leave, but barely two steps away, I came to a sudden halt. Stars shot out from behind my eyes, and the room started to tilt. I grabbed the wall for stability and sank down to the floor, waiting for the police to come.

But no one came. Even hours later. Had she not seen me?

Early this morning, feeling better, I put everything back the way I found it, like I was never even here—like the way Mom and me used to clean up before my father got home from work.

"Get every crumb," she'd say. "Chairs need to be tucked beneath the table, ten inches apart. No streak lines when you wash the cabinets: smooth, smooth, smooth. Daddy doesn't like a mess. Everything needs to be spick-and-span."

Luckily, every time I puked, it landed on the tarp. I rolled it up, glanced out the window, and that's when I saw her.

Day.

She was headed this way, holding a bag in her hand. I backed away from the window, keeping my eye on the knob, waiting for it to turn, flashing forward to what I would say.

But she didn't come in.

I saw her walking away again, her fists tucked into the pockets of her jacket.

While she went back inside the house, I opened the door. Inside the bag was more food than I'd had in days—granola bars, applesauce, bananas, a loaf of bread—as well as a couple of bottles of water.

But there was something else too. An envelope. A note for me?

I opened it up.

I would like to talk to you about your case. I'll be back later today.

At the bottom of the bag was a pad of paper and a pen. Does she expect me to write her back? Nothing makes sense. Who is this girl? Why isn't she calling the police? What could possibly be in it for her?

twelve

It's after school, and the bag of food is still hanging on the door handle of the barn, which means he either a) left last night or b) has yet to come out of the barn.

I'm assuming the first option is the correct one. I mean, at this point he's got to suspect that I'm onto him, so why risk sticking around?

I approach the barn door, pretending to be talking on the phone. "No, that's fine," I mutter into the voice piece, feeling stupid for doing so, but if he *is* still here, I don't want him to know that I'm totally alone.

Rain droplets pelt against my face. I mutter a few more words. Meanwhile, a swarm of questions storm inside my head: What will I ask first? Why didn't I think to make a list? What if he doesn't want me butting in?

I take another step, trying to get a grip, but my pulse races and my insides shake. I peer over my shoulder to make sure that no one's lurking behind me, and then I grab the bag, hating the noise it makes: the crinkle of plastic, the jostling of containers.

I look inside it. My heart instantly clenches. The container I used for the sandwich appears to be empty. The granola bars are gone, and so are the bananas, my envelope, and the notebook and pen.

There's a folded-up note. He wrote me back. Should I read what it says? Or knock on the door?

I close my eyes, reminding myself that my mom has always been notorious for this kind of thing—getting to the bottom of questionable cases, that is. But does that help ease my anxiety?

A big. Fat. Walloping. No.

"Hey, Sunshine," a voice shouts from behind, making me jump.

I swivel around to look, hearing a gasp escape from my throat.

It's Dad. He crosses the yard, trampling through the fallen leaves. "Sorry if I startled you." He wraps his arms around me.

I hold him close, pressing my nose into the nylon of his

jacket; he smells different somehow—like cinnamon breath mints. "It's really good to see you," I tell him. It's been almost a week.

He takes a step back, breaking the embrace moments too soon. His hair looks shorter than normal, like he just got it cut; it's been purposely messed up with gel, rather than parted to the side in his usual dad do. His clothes are different too—his jeans are darker; his shirt's snugger against his chest.

"Your mother's working late tonight," he says.

"How do you know? Did you come to see her?" I can hear the hope in my voice, can feel the desperation in my heart.

"I came to see *you*." He smiles birthday-cake wide, as if that's the answer I want to hear. "Your mom and I were texting earlier and she mentioned a late meeting, so I brought dinner. Sound good?"

Before I can answer, he motions to the bag I'm holding.

"What's that?" he asks. "And what were you doing? Did I interrupt you from something?" He looks toward the barn door.

"Nothing." I shrug, tucking the bag behind my back, as if he can no longer see it. "I was just cleaning up some stuff."

"Cleaning... *right*." He kicks a pile of leaves. "I imagine you've worked up quite an appetite."

"Definitely." I nod and follow him inside, into the dining room, where he's already cleared the table. The familiar white tote from Tuchi's Thai House is sitting on the buffet. While Dad unloads it, I place the bag beneath my chair, out of eyeshot, and begin setting the table.

He's ordered all of my and Mom's favorites: fried lemongrass tofu, drunken garlic noodles, sweet-and-sour spring rolls, and caramelized eggplant dumplings. He also got us extra white rice and Tuchi's famous sticky peanut sauce.

"This looks incredible," I say, taking a seat and piling up my plate.

Dad sits across from me and lights a candle.

"What's the occasion?" I ask.

"Do we need an occasion for candle-lighting?"

"Normally? Yes. A birthday, a power outage..."

"How about we change that policy?" He winks. "How about we light a lot more candles." He opens the wrapper on his package of chopsticks, and instantly I get a gnawing sensation in my gut.

Because he never uses chopsticks.

Because Mom and I would always offer to teach him, explaining that part of the culinary experience is eating with the utensils of the country of the food's origin. But still he'd always insist on a fork.

So, what's the difference now? And when did he start winking?

"It's been a while since we had Thai food, hasn't it?" He smiles.

I nod, unable to take my eyes off the way he holds the sticks, incorporating his thumb and ring finger. He's no longer wearing his wedding band. There's a mark on his skin in its place—a blank white circle.

He smiles wider, even though he's not supposed to be happy. "I've missed our Thai nights."

We used to order Thai food most Friday nights; it was our way of starting the weekend right. But that was all BS (Before the Separation, that is), four weeks and five days ago now.

"So," he begins, "how have things been around here? Anything exciting going on?"

I'm tempted to tell him about Julian, especially considering that Dad's entire career revolves around mentoring people from all walks of life. Dad himself came up with the organization's acronym: SHINE (Second chances, Honoring each individual, Instilling dignity, Nurturing talent, Equality for all).

I open my mouth to broach the topic, but before I can utter a sound, music starts to play—an old '80s song, something about a rose having a thorn. . . .

Dad fishes inside his pocket for his phone. A new ringtone. A shiny metallic case.

"What happened to your boring beep?"

"If you haven't noticed, I'm trying to put the brakes on boring." Dad checks the screen and mutes the song.

"Anything important?"

"Nothing that can't wait while I'm having dinner with my number-one girl." Another stupid grin.

I hide the revulsion on my face with a giant bite of broccoli.

"So, tell me, I almost forgot," he says, "how did your first Peace & Justice meeting go? Did you already have it?"

"It was yesterday, actually."

His phone vibrates against the table. Someone left a message. He checks the screen again. Meanwhile, I try to tell him about the lack of interest at my meeting, but barely three sentences in, he cuts me off, reminding me how Mom had stormed the state house at the ripe old age of twelve, demanding stricter laws on animal testing.

"And they actually sat back and listened to her." He laughs. "Your mom...she was a firecracker right out the gate. You should've seen her in grad school: everyone wanted in on her action—on whatever cause she stood behind. That kind of fire...it's magnetic."

And apparently I don't have it.

"Sounds like you miss her," I say.

He looks at me. His smile falls flat. "I miss the way things used to be—here, with all of us."

"Does that mean you'll be coming home soon?" I can already tell that it doesn't.

Dad reaches for something else in his pocket—a handful

of cash, of all things. He slides it across the table at me—five ten-dollar bills. "Since I haven't been around to give you an allowance," he says.

"Since when have I gotten an allowance?"

"Use it toward your Peace & Justice mission."

"Thanks," I say, staring at the long string of numbers and letters across one of the bills, wishing it were a code that I could crack—something to make sense of all that's going on. "But this doesn't answer my question about you coming home."

He stares at me for five long seconds without uttering a single sound. It's in that silence that the truth becomes clear: He isn't coming home. He doesn't ever want to come home. "I love you and I love your mother."

"But..." I say, feeling my heart strings tighten.

"But I think it's better if your mom and I part ways for a while."

I swallow down the truth, almost wishing that I could take the question back, that I could un-hear his horrible answer.

"Of course that doesn't mean I'm parting from you," he continues.

"There's something I need to tell you," I blurt, still thinking about Julian. Maybe that will bring Dad home.

"There's something I need to tell you too." His eyes go funeral-serious. His mouth is a straight, tense line.

My stomach drops, already anticipating the worst. I cross my fingers beneath my chair—the way I did when I was five—as if it will bring me luck.

"I found an apartment," he says.

"And?" I ask, already knowing the answer, but I need a moment. This is happening way too fast.

"And I put down a deposit."

"So you're no longer staying at the motel?"

"Better than the motel." His face brightens. "I'll be right downtown, near one of your favorite places . . . the independent movie theater. Maybe you'll use some of that money to see a show and then come visit me."

I scoot back in my chair, trying to digest what all of this means.

"I know." His voice softens. "This probably wasn't what you wanted to hear. But you have to understand; it has nothing to do with you."

I hate the tone of his voice. I hate his Dr. Phil–speak even more. I just want to hit STOP, press REWIND, and go back ten years—to my six-year-old princess-themed birthday party, when everything was just horse-drawn carriages and Cinderella castles. "Does Mom know?"

"About the apartment?"

"About the fact that you're no longer wearing your wedding ring, and that you're not ever coming home."

He lets out a sigh, but he doesn't deny any of it. "I wanted to talk to you first." He picks up his chopsticks and begins plucking at noodles, trying to make things normal, except the noodles never make it to his mouth.

"Normal for you is a fork," I snap.

Dad makes a face; he doesn't understand. We're not speaking the same language.

My phone chirps. I check the screen. It's a text from Mom. Her ears must be burning. "Mom will be home in less than an hour," I tell him, though I thought she was working late. Is she cutting things short to see him? "Will you be sticking around to see her?"

He peeks at his watch (a braided leather band, a bronze face; it must be new as well). "I can't tonight."

"Why am I not surprised?"

"Look, Day..." There's yet another grin on his face, as if there's anything even remotely grin-worthy going on. "You're a smart girl, but this isn't some Disney movie where the parents get back together in the end and everyone lives happily ever after."

"Then what's with this whole scene: the candlelit dinner, the surprise visit, the nice words about Mom..." I set my phone to burst mode to take shots of him—in his new clothes and with his new hair—holding a pair of chopsticks the wrong way.

"What are you doing?"

"Capturing this moment."

"I won't have you disrespecting me."

"And I won't sit here while you patronize *me*. I deserve more than spring rolls and a wad of cash. Thank you for the food, but I've lost my appetite." I go up to my room and shut the door.

He doesn't follow.

thirteen

I sit down on the edge of the bed and wait for a knock on my door. When it doesn't come, I take my cell phone out of my pocket and flip through the pictures of Dad, trying to make sense of what just happened.

I focus in on one of them. The grin on his face looks forced. He's leaning back, as if somewhat at ease, even though nothing about our conversation was easy.

I go to my computer and upload the photo, setting it on the screen beside a handful of older photos—one from Christmas, several years back: Mom and Dad sitting on the sofa. Dad's wearing a lumpy sweater. His hair is perfectly parted to the side. He looks so happy, leaning in toward Mom, his eyes focused on her smile.

There's also a picture from the camping trip we took the summer I turned thirteen: Mom and Dad snuggled by the fire, unaware that I was looking on from the tent. Dad's got his lips pressed against Mom's cheek. His eyes are closed. There's a smile curled across Mom's lips.

I open yet another folder and move my cursor over a photo taken a couple of summers ago: Mom and Dad sitting at opposite ends of a porch swing, angled away from each other, faking awkward smiles for the camera. Beside it there's a picture from this past July: Mom's sitting by herself at the picnic table, staring off into space, while Dad stands idle only a couple of feet away.

When did he stop trying to make things better?

When did they both start forcing smiles?

I move to stand in front of my mirror to take a picture of myself: this person who doesn't see, this girl who's been so naive.

There's a door slam downstairs. I go across the hall to look out the bathroom window—to watch Dad get into his car, start the engine, and pull away, driving right over my heart.

I head downstairs. The food's been cleaned up, but the bag from the shed remains tucked beneath my chair. Dad obviously didn't see it; he must've been in a hurry. The reality of that helps dry my tears.

Back up in my room, I pluck the note out of the bag and open up the folds.

Thanks for the food (and the place to stay). As you probably guessed by now, I followed you home from the train depot. I can't really make up a worthy excuse as to why—at least not one that won't make me sound like a creep.

I didn't intend to stay, and I would've left by now, but I got sick while I was here. I was going to leave this morning, but your note stopped me.

I'm curious why you want to talk about the case. If you change your mind, that's fine. If not, you know where to find me—for the next few hours anyway.

I read the letter one more time, feeling my skin chill.

My phone chirps. It's a text from Mom: Just another 20 min and I'm leaving—promise! Is Dad still there??? Xoxo!

I flop back onto my bed and gaze up at the ceiling, unsure what to call this feeling. Insecurity? Anger? Frustration? Fear? All of those emotions roll up into a ball and wedge beneath my ribs, making it hard to breathe.

My cell phone rings ("The Chicken Dance"). I check the screen. It's Tori. "Hey," I answer.

"So?"

"So *what?*"

"Are you kidding? I didn't want to bring it up at lunch—in case Jeannie really *does* like him; she can be such a mysterious mouse at times—and then you took off so fast after school today, I didn't even get to ask..."

"*What?*"

"Max...after the meeting yesterday...dish."

"There's not too much to dish about. He drove me home. I invited him inside for a glass of water, and then he left."

"Was there tongue?"

"Seriously?"

"Friends can play tongue tag, you know. No judgment."

"I refuse to have this conversation."

"You don't find him even the slightest bit good-looking?"

"Sure, he's good-looking. But why do I need to have a boyfriend?"

"Who said anything about boy*friend*. How about a boy*toy*?"

"There are way more important things in life than toys."

"Like what? Saving the world?" She yawns. "You can't cuddle up with that at night, you know. Humans need love and companionship, in addition to a sense of personal fulfillment."

"Have you been reading your mother's self-help books again?"

"Do I sound wiser for it?"

"No, you just sound more annoying." I sit up and gaze out

the window, startled to see Julian outside. There's a water bottle in his hand. He's going for the hose. "Can I call you later?"

"Have I inspired you to give Max a booty call?"

"What do you think?"

"Call me later."

I hang up, pocket my phone, and grab my camera. I head into the living room, where the view into the backyard is best.

Shielded by the curtain, I can see him clearly. Julian is crouched behind a stack of firewood, drinking from the hose, with his back toward me. His hair is chin-length and wavy, the color of chocolate kisses. His pants look even bigger now than just days ago. They hang low on his hips, exposing the small of his back. He angles toward me, slightly, and I zoom in with my camera lens, able to make out the sharpness of his cheekbones and the dimple in his chin. He uses the water to wash his face, to wet his hands, to run his fingers through his hair. The front of his T-shirt gets soaked. Water drips down the center of his chest, making a beeline toward his abdomen.

He must be absolutely chilled. Meanwhile, my face flashes hot. I shouldn't be doing this. This is an invasion of his privacy. Still, I take several snapshots, inspired to set them beside the photos from the train depot—to see if his shoulders look just as broad; to check if his skin resembles the color of apple butter, the way it does now.

I go to zoom in a little closer.

But then his eyes snap open.

And he looks in my direction.

I duck behind the window, feeling my heart pound.

My phone chirps again. I pluck it out of my pocket. It's another message from Mom: *Im so sorry! Is Dad still there? We r so close to getting Pandora home!!! Just one more hour.*

Just one more hour.

Just twenty more minutes.

Just two more days and *"I'll be done with this case, this plight, this violation of justice."*

But minutes turn into hours. And days turn into weeks. Meanwhile, we're becoming more and more like tenants who inhabit the same space rather than mother and daughter.

I peek back at Julian as he rolls up the hose, thinking how I've never been one to keep things from my parents. But nothing is the same now. This "separation" feels more like a wide, gaping hole.

My stomach growls. I need to eat. There's no sense wasting good Thai food. I'm sure Julian's hungry too. I head into the kitchen to fix us both a plate.

fourteen

fourteen

Plate of food in hand, I head out to the barn, my nerves absolutely shot. Standing at the door, I knock a couple of times, but it makes no sound.

I try again, slightly louder.

The door opens. Julian's standing there. He towers over me by at least six inches. His golden-brown eyes focus hard on mine, stealing my thoughts, blanking my mind. And suddenly I have no words.

I hand him the plate of food. There's a confused expression knotted up on his face.

"I thought you might be hungry." I shove my hands into my pockets, one hand wrapping around the pepper spray, the other clutching my cell phone.

He opens the door wider to let me in.

I step inside, feeling the rush of my adrenaline. "So, I've been researching your case."

"*Why?*" He closes the door behind me.

"Because you were here, loitering around my house and staying inside my barn."

"So how come you didn't call the police?"

"I *did* call them. And I'll call them again if I have to."

He takes a step closer, as if to challenge me. "How come you're not calling them right now?"

"Because maybe I want to learn more about your case," I say, trying my best to sound brave. "Maybe the details of your arrest don't add up for me."

"How do I know you won't turn me in—that whatever I say won't be used against me?"

"You don't." I swallow hard. "But if you *aren't* guilty, or if the case *is* being mishandled, then I want to try to help."

His expression turns cold: a vacant, unblinking stare. "Need I remind you that I've been accused of an unspeakable crime?"

"No reminders necessary. I'm aware of the allegations."

"You're committing a crime too, you know—by helping me."

I can feel my face turn pink, and can feel the dark red hives around my neck. "Are you planning on turning me in?"

"Your parents can't possibly know I'm here. They'd ground you for good."

"You might be surprised about that one."

"Oh, yeah? Why's that?"

Droplets of sweat form at my brow. "Do you want my help or not?"

"What's in it for you?"

"I'm not looking for anything."

"Everybody's always looking for something." He takes another step closer.

But I don't budge an inch. "What are you still doing here? Why aren't you at least a hundred miles away by now?"

The question takes him off guard. I can tell by his body language. He looks downward. His posture angles away. "I already told you: I got sick."

"But still... That can't be the only reason. Why aren't you in Canada or something?"

He turns to set the plate down. "I guess I was kind of hoping that in the time I'm laying low, new information would surface in my case, exonerating me."

I bite my lip, focusing hard on *him* now, trying to decide if he's being honest. "Well, maybe, with your help, I'll be able to find that new information."

"You don't even know if I'm innocent."

"I'm going to assume you are—until I prove otherwise, that is."

He comes closer again, standing just inches from me now. "And then what?"

"And then I'll call the police back." I pull my cell phone out of my pocket for no apparent reason. My hand shakes. My face burns. "We can start tomorrow. Are you in?"

He looks away again. Meanwhile, my mouth turns dry and my heart won't stop hammering.

"Well?" I ask, trying to feign indifference.

His breath has quickened; I can tell from the motion in his chest.

"I'm in," he says, finally.

fifteen

It isn't until after eleven that my mother finally comes home.

"Day?" she calls out.

I hear the clank of her keys as she drops them on the table in the entryway. The floorboards creak as she makes her way up the stairs. I quickly minimize the screen on my computer—the list of questions I'm drafting for Julian—and go into my virtual gallery, making it look like I'm arranging photos.

"Sweetie?" she says. There's a light rap on my open door. "What's this...working on a Friday night?"

"Like mother, like daughter."

"Well, how about a peace offering?"

I turn to look. She's holding a box from Brewer's Bakery.

"I got us some red velvet cupcakes," she says. "Your favorite."

I swivel back around to my screen. "Isn't it you who always says it isn't good to eat after seven?" Something about the body not having sufficient time for proper digestion.

"Couldn't we make an exception, just this once?"

I move my cursor over a photo of a girl I saw at the park. I snuck the shot on a walk home with Jeannie a few weeks ago. I asked Jeannie to pose in front of the swirly slide. Little did she know that I was missing her entirely, zooming in on the girl just over her shoulder.

In the photo, the girl is sitting on a bench with her boyfriend. He's caught in a laugh with his mouth arched wide. She's smiling too, but it's clearly forced. Her eyes look teary and her posture's pointed away from him. I drag the photo under a heading that says "Alone with Other People."

"I know you're upset," Mom begins. "I haven't been available much."

But...

"But you have to know," she continues, "I'm doing some very important work."

"More important than being home with your family?"

"Not *more* important, just different-important. Was Dad upset?"

"*I* was upset. Doesn't that count for anything?"

"I'm sorry." She sighs, coming farther into the room. She sits down on my bed. "I know this has been an adjustment for you too."

"It has," I say, thinking how ever since her and Dad's separation—leaving a wide, gaping hole in our musketeer trio—Mom and I have been on two entirely separate pages: she, distracted by work; me, in a trio of one (which makes absolutely no sense, which is why it doesn't work).

"I never got to ask: How did your Peace & Justice meeting go? It was yesterday, wasn't it?"

"It didn't go as well as I'd hoped."

"Did you have a nice turnout?"

"Define *nice*."

"Ten? Fifteen people?"

"Try three, including Jeannie and Tori." I pivot in my seat to face her.

"Sounds like you'll just have to work harder."

"I already *do* work hard."

Mom snickers. "I once had to work eighteen-hour days for five weeks straight, and that still wasn't 'hard work' enough."

"When will this household be your hard work?"

"Excuse me?" Mom's jaw stiffens. Her eyes narrow.

"Sometimes I feel like I need to get locked up in jail if I want to see you ever."

"Don't take your failed meeting out on me." She gets up and leaves the room.

But I'm not done fighting yet. I grab my folders full of Peace & Justice plans: my meeting's agenda, the articles I found concerning various human rights movements (for fair trade, free love, environmental justice), the extra posters I made up, and the research I did on similar clubs at other schools. I barrel down the stairs and storm into the kitchen. Mom's at the stove. I drop everything onto the table with a satisfying thud. "Do you still think I haven't been working hard enough?"

But Mom continues to stir her pot, refusing to turn around.

"*Tell me*," I shout, desperate for a reaction. "This is a month's worth of research right here...."

Mom shakes her head. *Stir, stir, stir.*

"Nothing I do is ever good enough, is it?" I continue. "Is that why you barely come home? Why you hole yourself up in your office for hours on end? Why we never talk anymore?"

Stir, stir.

"Do I remind you too much of Dad?" I blurt, grasping at straws. "He was here today. Where were you? How come you're not even trying to make this family work?"

Still she doesn't answer, which makes tears well up in my eyes. Why am I not even worthy of a fight?

I reach into my pocket for my phone. I take a picture of her back as she stands at the stove, sampling whatever's in the pot with her wooden spoon. I can see her reflection against the microwave door. Her face is neither sad nor angry. Her eyebrows furrow as she smacks her lips together and then adds more salt.

Like I'm not even here.

Like hot bubbling tears aren't streaking down my face.

I turn the camera lens on me and take a snapshot of myself, with my puffy eyes and my blotchy cheeks. I imagine the two photos in an album, side by side, under a heading that says "Dysfunction."

When Mom still doesn't say anything, I gather up all of my Peace & Justice paraphernalia and go for the door, making a beeline for the trash cans, assuming she'll try to stop me or change my mind.

She doesn't.

I waited until early morning before going out to see what Day had thrown into the trash.

Poster boards stuck out from beneath a trash can lid. I grabbed one and held it up in the moonlight: the letters PB&J were huge across the front. The date was listed too. I'd been on the run for almost two weeks.

I pulled a couple of folders out as well, picking through old banana peels and a bunch of other half-eaten crap too gross to salvage. A stream of papers blew out from one of the folders. I scooted down to pick them up, just as a light shined in my direction.

I dropped everything. And looked up.

It was Day. She aimed her flashlight straight into my eyes.

I stood, holding my hands up like I was suddenly under arrest. "I heard you," I attempted to explain. "That is, I saw you throwing this stuff away."

She was dressed in a robe and slippers, and some sort of long silky pants.

"I'll leave if you want," I told her.

She looked away instead of answering. Her hair blew back in the wind, away from her face, revealing skin that seemed to glisten. "I shouldn't have dumped this stuff," she said. "It was a bad decision in the heat of the moment."

I've made enough of those.

She put away her pistol of a flashlight and scooted down to take her things. I scooted down too, trying to help, able to smell her—a mix of vanilla and cinnamon, like something out of a bakery.

She paused to look at my wrist—at the tattoo of the pickax on the underside. I watched her stare at it, unable to tell what she was thinking. Finally she met my eyes again, but instead of showing fear, her expression seemed softer somehow. The tension in her mouth had melted. The muscles around her eyes were relaxed. Maybe I'd been locked up for too long, but she was the most beautiful thing I'd ever seen.

I looked away again, stood up, and handed her a stack of folders. "I should go," I said, peering back at the barn.

"I was actually hoping you might want to get started now, since we're both up."

"Get started?"

"With your case."

Right. My case. I think I nodded. I'm pretty sure she said "great."

She came to the barn not long after, carrying a couple of tote bags. She pulled a jacket from one of them, held it up to my chest, and then forced it into my hands. "I have others if it doesn't fit. My dad is a regular at yard sales."

She took out a blanket next, explaining that she'd knitted it in the eighth grade as part of a fund-raising event for the children's hospital. "It was just sitting in my room," she explained. "I'm happy it'll actually get some use."

I lifted the blanket up to my face, without even thinking. It smelled like her—that vanilla-bean scent.

"Thank you again for salvaging my stuff from the trash," she said. "I'm kind of embarrassed, actually . . . that you heard my mother and me fighting." Her face turned bright pink. "I was kind of being a brat—not exactly one of my prouder moments."

The comment took me off guard, because if she was embarrassed for fighting with her mother, then I should've been mortified for ending up in juvie.

She opened another bag and took out a bunch of stuff— soap, hand towels, napkins, food supplies—setting it all on a toolbox. She held up a can of tuna. "I heard this was a personal favorite of yours. The only problem is that I didn't know if you preferred freshwater or oil-packed. Do tell. Inquiring minds want to know."

"Oil, for the fat. Believe it or not, small cans pack big protein—at least in the case of tuna."

"Good to know." She nodded like she actually gave a shit.

"And now my inquiring mind wants to know: Why are you doing this? Giving me clothes, food, and water, and letting me use this place as shelter? You don't even know me."

"I actually don't know any of the people who receive my charity."

"Is that what I am to you? A charitable cause?"

She shrugged like the term was no big deal—like there was no shame in getting help. "Would you prefer it if I called you something else?"

"How about a felon? That seems the most obvious choice."

She let out a sigh. "I technically can't call you that if you haven't been proven guilty."

"Who are you?"

Her face messed up in confusion. "What do you mean?"

"I mean, who are you?"

We were standing just inches apart, and I had no idea how we'd gotten that way. Had she moved closer? Had I? Would it have been too obvious if I stepped back? She could sense the awkwardness too—I could tell because she suddenly didn't *know where to look. Her gaze flicked back and forth between the stuff she brought and the door to the barn before finally resting on my chest. There was a smear of something red in the corner of her mouth. Strawberry jam? Residual toothpaste? I wanted more than anything to wipe it with my thumb.*

I backed up, looked away, and threw the blanket down on a toolbox. I didn't want to smell it. I didn't want to feel this. She needed to go. I needed some space. "I have to get some sleep."

"I thought we were going to get started." She pulled a tape recorder from her pocket—one of those handheld ones—and explained that she wanted to tape our conversations. "That way, I can go over the details of the case as many times as I need to."

I hated the idea—the possibility that she could use my words against me. My father was always using my mother's words against her:

"You promised you were going to stop taking pills."

"You said you were going to clean this house."

"You told me you were going to make sure the kids wore their seat belts."

I don't trust words—not my parents', nor my own.

sixteen

sixteen

I place the tape recorder on the bale of hay between us and pull a list of questions from my pocket. Instantly he withdraws, backing away, avoiding eye contact.

"I'm not going to share this with anyone," I tell him.

"Even if I say something that could pin me? Or reveal a clue that could possibly exonerate me? Then, seriously, what's the point?"

He's right. There would be no point. "You're just going to have to trust me," I say, looking toward the side of his face.

His jaw is locked. His lips look tense. "I don't really trust anyone."

"Did you trust your parents?"

He shakes his head. "I especially didn't trust them."

I take a deep breath, thinking how no matter what information I'm able to dig up, this case isn't just about his guilt or innocence. He lost both his parents in a really traumatic way. "I'd like to try to help you," I tell him. "But if you've changed your mind, that's okay too. You can leave by tonight. I never saw you here."

"I want your help," he says, quickly, quietly.

"Okay, then I'm going to have to record our conversations."

It's silent between us for several seconds, which I totally understand. I mean, he doesn't even know me. What reason does he have to give me his trust? Except for the fact that I haven't turned him in yet.

"Let's go," he says, nodding to the tape recorder.

I push RECORD before he can change his mind.

ME: Where were you on Saturday, May 4th, the day of your parents' deaths?

JULIAN: I mowed my neighbor's yard first thing in the morning, around ten. After that, I drove to Dover Beach; that was at noon.

ME: Did you come home between mowing the lawn and going to the beach?

JULIAN: Yes, but I didn't change.

ME: You went to the beach in your mowing clothes?

JULIAN: Yeah. I was wearing a pair of shorts and a T-shirt. I don't go to the beach to suntan. Plus, it was May—too cold to swim. I just like to sit on the rocks and write. Sometimes I also read. I've kept a journal for most of my life.

ME: How long did you stay at Dover Beach?

JULIAN: Until four thirty or five.

ME: Did you see anyone while you were there?

JULIAN: I did. A girl named Ariana. We bumped into each other.

ME: So, you have an alibi.

JULIAN: I thought I did. Ariana said she saw me there too, but then the police got her all confused. By the time she was done talking to them, she didn't know if it was Saturday or Sunday that she saw me.

ME: How about the security cameras? I know that Dover Beach has them.

JULIAN: They do, but they only caught me there on Sunday.

ME: Were you there Sunday too?

JULIAN: Yep.

ME: And how about Ariana?

JULIAN: She was there both days.

ME: Did the camera catch her there both days?

JULIAN: Yep again. I should add: I later learned that one of the security cameras was broken.

ME: Which one?

JULIAN: The one in the far left corner of the parking lot.

ME: Is that where you bumped into Ariana?

JULIAN: No. I saw her by the showers.

ME: But you weren't taking a shower.

JULIAN: I was just walking by that area when I bumped into her.

ME: Did the police talk to others who were at the beach on that date—anyone else who might've confirmed that you were there? Or did you order any food at the snack bar? Might you have a receipt?

JULIAN: Negative. To all of the above.

ME: And nothing out of the ordinary happened while you were there?

JULIAN: Nope.

ME: Okay, so you left the beach around four thirty or five. What did things look like when you got home?

JULIAN: Just like normal, I guess.

ME: Did it appear as though someone had broken in?

JULIAN: No.

ME: Is this too hard for you?

JULIAN: It's just a lot—picturing everything, remembering my mom like that.

ME: And your dad?

JULIAN: . . .

ME: Do you want to take a break?

JULIAN: No, it's fine. Keep going.

ME: Who do you think killed your father?

JULIAN: . . .

ME: Julian?

JULIAN: I think my mother did it.

ME: But investigators say no?

JULIAN: They think she was too weak to be able to strike my father over the head with the kind of force that caused his brain hemorrhage.

ME: And what do *you* think?

JULIAN: I think people are capable of a lot when they're really pissed off.

ME: Are you cold?

JULIAN: . . .

ME: You're shaking.

JULIAN: I'm fine. Really.

ME: Why do you think your mother killed your father?

JULIAN: Why does anyone kill? Because they want that person dead.

ME: Did your mother want your father dead?

JULIAN: Yes.

ME: How do you know?

JULIAN: She told me—many times, actually.

ME: According to police reports, your mother was found in the bathtub with the water still running. Did you find her?

JULIAN: Uh-huh.

ME: And there was something in the reports about pre-scription medication. . . .

JULIAN: Yep. She'd recently taken enough to gag a horse.

ME: Do you think she took them on purpose? Or by accident?

JULIAN: Hard to accidentally swallow an extra twenty-seven pills.

ME: Could someone have forced her to take that many?

JULIAN: Yeah, it's called her inner demon—the same demon that made her slit her wrists twice.

ME: Didn't she ever get help?

JULIAN: She was seeing a therapist at one point. You can see how well that worked out for her.

ME: And after that?

JULIAN: She said that therapists were a waste of her time.

ME: So, how did she keep getting pills?

JULIAN: Who says she was getting them legally?

ME: Did your father know about any of this ... her slashed wrists, the illegal medication, or her attempts to get help?

JULIAN: ...

ME: You're shaking again. Do you need to grab a blanket?

JULIAN: ...

ME: Do you want to take that break?

JULIAN: That's probably a good idea.

seventeen

seventeen

I spend the following day trying to catch up on schoolwork, but failing miserably because I can't stop thinking about Julian's case. At night, I toss and turn in bed, unable to sleep. There are way too many questions bouncing around inside my head:

Why didn't Julian trust his parents?

Why did the surveillance cameras only catch him at the beach on Sunday rather than Saturday, when they caught Ariana there on both days?

Is it true that Mrs. Roman really wanted her husband dead? And, if so, why?

I try to distract myself with thoughts of happy-funny times—like Halloween, two Octobers ago, when Tori showed up at Lesley Thibodeau's party dressed as a tampon, even though it wasn't a costume party.

I didn't really know Tori back then. To me she was just the pink-haired girl in my study hall that always doodled geisha girls on the covers of her notebooks and wore mismatched socks. But I still tried to help her out that day (not that her tampon-wearing self really needed it) by giving her my sweater to break up all that white. Unfortunately the sweater was red, and so she ended up looking like a used tampon, which was sort of gross and funny at the same time—at least, it was funny to us.

Needless to say, we didn't last long at the party, but that turned out to be perfectly okay, because we laughed the entire way to Dino's, where we fit right in beside a busload of senior citizens after their Halloween-costume-wearing bingo night party. Tori and I ordered root beer floats and a basketful of onion rings, and really got to know each other.

We've been close ever since. As nutty as she can be, she often has the enviable ability of seeing the world through a crystal-clear lens, which is why I should've called her last night instead of losing it on my mom and throwing away all my meeting stuff.

I roll over in bed and stare out the window. The light from the moon casts over me like a blanket. A soft breeze filters in through the open crack. In textbook terms, this is an optimum night for sleep. And yet I couldn't feel more restless.

"Day?" Mom knocks lightly on the door.

I sit up, just as she comes in.

"Is it safe in here?" she asks.

"Safe?"

"Yes. Is this a war-free zone?"

"I don't want to fight," I tell her. "But I also don't want to be ignored."

Mom sits on the edge of the bed. Her hair's pulled back in a messy heap. Aside from a trip to the grocery store, she's been working in her office all day. "I didn't feel like I had much choice. You weren't acting rationally last night—at least not for a serious discussion."

"Do all of your serious discussions involve cupcake-shaped Band-Aids?"

She smirks. "I guess I deserved that. I'm sorry I haven't been so available lately. That's what this is about, isn't it...rather than your less-than-successful club meeting?"

"It's about everything." I sigh. "Dad and I were waiting for you to have dinner with us last night."

Her jaw stiffens and she looks away. "I doubt that he was waiting."

"Since when are you Miss Insecurity?"

"It's just that your dad seems happier on his own."

"Are *you* happier?"

She repositions on the bed. Her eyes fill up with tears; the sight of them takes me aback, because Mom has always been the confident one—so courageous and unbreakable.

"Work helps keep me distracted from worrying too much about happiness," she says. "It also gives me a sense of value— like what I'm doing is really meaningful. But the deeper I dig into my work, the more needed I become. There are people really counting on me, Day. And I know that you're counting on me too. It's just... It's hard to find a balance, you know?"

I reach out to touch her forearm, thinking how tiny and fragile she looks all of a sudden, like a little girl, rather than the pillar of strength I've grown so accustomed to standing behind.

"I'm sorry," she says again, taking my hand, wrapping her fingers around my palm. "For not being around, for getting emotional like this."

"It's human to get emotional," I tell her. "You should try it more often."

She moves to give me a hug. I stroke her back, grateful for this moment. This is the most human I've ever seen her, and so I take a mental picture, reminding myself, once again, that no story is complete without listening to all sides.

eighteen

eighteen

"Day?" my mother calls.

"Just a second," I holler back.

It's Sunday morning, I'm in my room, working on my list of questions to ask Julian.

"Breakfast is ready!" she calls again.

I get up and head downstairs. Mom's loaded up a serving dish with stacks of French toast; they're dripping with maple syrup. There's also a separate plate of sausage links.

"What's the special occasion?" I ask her, suddenly feeling on high alert.

"How about hunger?" She motions for me to take a seat at

the kitchen island, beside her. She looks way too put-together for just a lazy Sunday at home. She's showered and changed. Her hair's been freshly flat-ironed and there's a subtle layer of pink shimmer on her lids and cheeks. Her phone sits on the island, between us—the third wheel in our party of two.

I fork off a piece of my French toast and take a bite. The thick wad of syrupy goodness all but melts in my mouth. "Did you somehow channel Paula Dean to make this?"

"Not good?"

"More like *delectable*."

"Really?" She straightens up on her stool. "Go, me!"

I spoon a couple of the sausages onto my plate, noticing the suspicious pale brown color. "Real?"

"What do you think?"

Tofu; I'm sure of it. I can tell by the super-shiny casing. Mom likes to think of herself as a health nut, but in reality the majority of our meals come out of a cardboard box.

"Are you working today?" I ask, already anticipating the answer.

"Not if I can help it. Maybe one video conference call. Two at the most." She checks her phone for the time.

I take a sip of coffee, wondering if I only imagined our conversation last night. "How are you so sure that Syrian-prison Pandora is innocent? I mean, you've never even met her."

Mom's syrupy mouth drops open, her eyebrows shoot up,

and she lowers her fork to her plate with a clank. Shit, meet Fan. I've evidently hit a nerve.

"I may have never met her," Mom says, enunciating every syllable, "but that doesn't mean I haven't looked into her story, pulled it apart, consulted with the officials in charge of keeping her imprisoned. I've also talked to her family, friends, schoolteachers..."

"I get it," I say. Mom practices what she preaches, examining the facts from different angles—at least when it comes to her work. "It's just weird," I continue. "I mean, in theory, guilty people are supposed to get punished, but there are plenty that don't, thanks to plea deals, mishandled evidence, and different tiers of attorneys—from freebie public defenders to million-dollar lawyers who know how to work the system. In the end, where lies the truth? Thousands of dollars and hours later... do any of the players even care?"

"You're starting to sound like me." She taps her coffee mug against mine. "It's an imperfect system, which is why I'm working so hard to do my part. Believe me, if I didn't truly believe that Pandora was innocent, I wouldn't be working on her case." She checks her phone for the time once again. An entire minute has passed.

I eat my frustration with a bite of tofu sausage. It has the consistency of gummy bears, but not in a good way.

"So, what's on *your* agenda for today?" She's glaring at me now.

I peer out the window. The door to the barn is closed. She wouldn't have had reason to go out there this morning. Plus, she's not one for subtlety; she'd be far more direct if she knew or suspected something. "Why do you ask?"

"No reason. Just curious." Her eyebrows knit together and she gives me a puzzled grin.

I take a sip of coffee, trying to formulate my answer. But her phone rings before I can.

"It's Genevieve," she says, already off her stool. She holds up her finger, indicating that she'll only be a minute.

But I've heard that drill before.

While she heads to her office, I peek back out the window, wondering about Julian's truth. What is his version of what happened on the day his father was killed? The day he lost both his parents.

I woke up on the morning of October 6th knowing it was a good day to escape. I could feel it deep inside me—like an electrical current that charged through my veins, making me feel on fire.

I could barely sleep the night before, couldn't concentrate in classes on the day of, couldn't stomach a single morsel. Like the Christmas Eves you see on TV—kids tossing and turning in bed, unable to sleep a wink.

"Are you going to eat that pancake?" Jones asked. "If not, can I have it?"

Jones was fourteen years old, in juvie for stealing cars. I gave him my whole tray, too excited for food—giddy even, like I'd ever felt giddy about anything; never had any use for the word. Sort of ironic. It took me going to juvie to feel the excitement of Christmas.

It was drizzling, but we were still allowed to go outside for some fresh air. Stickney, the new guard, had been assigned to watch us—that was mistake number two. Mistake number one was that he'd been hired at all.

Stickney had his head so far up his ass that he couldn't see straight. I knew it. He knew it. He knew I knew it.

During the weeks that led up to the escape, I watched Stickney closely. Saw him flip out, royally, over Jordan's messy cell, ultimately pinning him to the ground (infraction: overreacting, resulting in a warning). I then saw him give a mere slap on the wrist when Williams jumped Douglas in the cafeteria, nearly knocking Douglas unconscious (infraction: underreacting, resulting in a meeting).

When Stickney started getting a little too social with the other inmates—detainees, we're called—by oversharing about his supposed hot ex-girlfriend and all his sexy conquests (most likely the product of his warped imagination), I knew his fate was sealed.

I had my way of letting him know that Big Brother was watching. Whenever he so much as sneezed in the wrong direction, I'd be there, eyes wide, silently judging. It got so that whenever he laughed too hard or did something shady— slipping a candy bar to Williams when he thought no one was looking, letting Jones skip morning classes for no reason other than he didn't feel like going, telling anybody who'd listen about some girl he'd been working at the bar he frequents— he'd look for me, checking to see if I'd noticed.

I always noticed.

Dad always noticed too—whenever Mom looked a little too happy or treated Steven's half of the room as anything other than a sacred shrine (collecting a pile of clothes on his bed or using his dresser to store extra bedsheets), Dad noticed and called her on it: Howdareyoudisrespect myson.Wipethatstupidsmileoffyoursmuglittleface.Whatis theretobehappyabout?Iwon'thaveyoudisrespectingthisfamily. Iworksohardwhileyousitaround.

The night before my escape from the detention center, I zeroed in on Byron Hensley, one of the newbies. I'd hand-picked Hensley for being thirteen years old, scared shitless, and way too pretty to stay safe around here. Other detainees had noticed him, and I knew that freaked him out. Sexually abused since he was five, Hensley sought revenge by murdering his mom and stepdad—or allegedly murdering them, like me.

Committing a crime like that at thirteen, I knew he was capable of acting out of desperation. I also suspected that he was just a wee bit crazy. I mean, who wouldn't be after growing up like that? Or committing a crime like that?

"You don't belong in here, man," I told him. "You should

totally plead insanity. They'll transfer you to a hospital. You won't even have to stand trial."

"The lawyer said something about that too," Hensley said, "but I got sent here instead. I think my hearing will decide if I'm sane enough for trial."

"So, show you're not sane."

"How do I do that?"

The wheels in my head started to turn. This would be easier than I thought. After a little coaching from me, the plan was set. Hensley's tears had dried up. He now had something to look forward to. Merry Christmas once again—I'd probably just given him his best gift. A temporary stint in a mental institution—until he received the proper meds and therapy that would magically turn him "sane" again—beat prison any day. At least that's what I told myself.

And so, there we were, a pack of nineteen of us, outside in the yard, getting some fresh air. Like most days, some of us were doing laps. Others were shooting baskets on the court or talking on the sidelines. A few more were playing a game of capture the flag, using an old sock as the flag.

Stickney was in the center of it all. One man, expected to have eyes in the back of his head: mistake number three.

I stood off to the side, by the fence that surrounded the yard. There was an area that curled around behind the building, out of eyeshot: mistake number four.

Was it a coincidence that a section of that fencing had been turned upward, just enough, where there'd been some construction going on? Or was that mistake number five?

Hensley gave me a nod and then kicked off his shoes, dropped his pants and boxers. He whipped off his T-shirt and started running around stark raving naked, singing "Santa Claus Is Coming to Town."

Stickney lost his shit. He blew his whistle, shouted at the top of his lungs, and started chasing Hensley around. But Hensley was too quick, skipping in circles, shaking his bare ass.

Other detainees started cheering, laughing, whistling, storming. Meanwhile, the bell rang, alerting us to line up and go in.

I bolted instead, slipping around to the side of the building. I'd planned on trying to scale the fence until I saw the damaged panel. I scooted beneath it. A jagged piece of the metal scratched my face, ripped my pants, and dug into my back. Blood ran down my cheek. But still I kept on running, never stopping to look back.

nineteen
nineteen

Roger Mason has this weird habit where he tears tiny scraps of paper from the pages of his notebook, chews them up into tight, round wads, and then collects them into a heap. When I first saw him doing it, I assumed he was making spitballs, but I soon stood corrected. Roger uses the saliva balls to erect various sculptures. I know this because he sits beside me in the library for every single B-Block. I even have a picture of his Eiffel Tower of balls.

It's B-Block now, and I'm trying to ignore the sound of him swishing paper around in his mouth, but it's so completely distracting, especially because he keeps sniffing up phlegm, like he has a bad cold, and so I can't help picturing snotty saliva balls. Normally it wouldn't bother me as much, but my nerves are shot. I'm so overtired.

Still, I'm using this study block to do research on Julian's case. According to another article I find, it seems that Julian was fairly well liked by his peers, even helping out the drama club by building sets. One classmate was quoted as saying that Julian "was a quiet guy, always writing in a journal. He never made any problems."

Another student said, "If I ever have a problem and need to talk stuff out, he's my first go-to."

Similarly, there are teachers and neighbors who claim to have been shocked by his arrest. "Something isn't right," said Madeline Romano, a recently retired English teacher at Julian's high school. "Julian is a gifted writer with a gentle soul. He was respectful in my class, and always worked well with his peers. I really think there's a major piece of this story that's missing."

"Hey, is that the Bates Motel?" a voice asks, from behind, instantly making me jump.

I swivel in my seat to find Tori.

"Whoa, looks like someone's a little on edge. Too much Red Bull in your Apple Jacks this morning?" She tsk-tsks before looking back at Roger's sculpture. "*Psycho*'s one of my all-time faves. Vince Vaughn as Norman Bates...totally hot, right? Though Anthony Perkins wasn't too shabby either.

Bonus points if you can re-create the infamous vacancy sign that stands in front of the motel."

Tori's got her hair in pigtails today, the tips of which match the bright gold stars on her knitted scarf. "Hey, there." She smiles at me. "Got a minute? I'm in major cri-cri mode."

"What's the crisis?" I ask. "Did Mr. Garblecki pass the history tests back?"

"Jarrod Koutsalakis is totally taking someone else to Hannah Hennelworth's 'It's-Saturday-let's-party' party."

"Oh, right. *That.*"

"Seriously?" She lets out an audible sigh. "Word's even spread to *you?*"

"Rest assured I actually have no idea what you're talking about. And, P.S., who is Hannah Hennelworth?"

Tori makes a confused face, her lips bunched up and her eyebrows knitted together. "How the hell am I supposed to know?"

"Well, you're going to her party, aren't you?"

"*Jarrod's* going." She rolls her eyes, frustrated that I can't keep up. "Apparently Hannah's some freshman girl who lives on the curve." (Note: the houses on the curve overlook the water and generally have their own servant quarters, which means that Hannah Hennelworth is rich—or at least that's the perception.) "Anyway, Hannah is having this party to put herself on the map."

"In other words, to buy people's friendship?"

Another eye roll. "You're totally missing the point here, Day."

"I'm not. Really. You want to go to the party, but Jarrod is taking someone else."

"Not just *some*one, *the* one. Becky Freaking Burkus. I mean, seriously, have you not noticed her skanky attire lately? Low-cut blouses, ho-length skirts, fishnet stockings, and visible string."

"As in shoelaces?"

"As in *G*," she barks, snagging the attention of Mr. Czarnecki, the librarian. "Becky's like a walking peep show," she whispers.

"And Jarrod's rumored to be dating that peep show. I must say, I'm kind of surprised to hear a boy has got you sinking to such shallow depths. I mean, honestly, using some girl for her curvy house party?"

Tori holds up her fist. "This is point." She waves her opposite hand in the air. "This is you." She passes her waving hand over the fisted point. "And this is you missing the point. Do I make myself clear?"

"Crystal."

Tori drags a chair in between Roger and me to sit. "Bottom line: we need to go to that party. Word is that Max is going to ask you."

"Okay, but I refuse to go to a party thrown by someone I

don't even know, whose intention it is to buy a bunch of shallow leeches—present company excluded, of course."

"Oh, come on, Ms. Scruples. Won't you even go for me? *Please?* I'll picket at your next save-the-kids/protect-the-rainforests/help-the-flying-squirrels rally." She bats her puppy dog eyes. "Remember that flying squirrels campaign last spring?" She giggles. "You had us planting trees everywhere."

"I'll think about it," I tell her.

"Well, think hard. I want to show up looking smokin' hot." She runs her palms over her red-and-white striped sweater.

I wonder if she knows how much her outfit looks like something out of Where's Waldo's closet.

"I'm so excited now." She claps silently and then glances at my computer screen. "Is that for the psych paper?"

"PB&J stuff, actually," I lie, feeling an instant ping of guilt.

"I already told you, PB&J belongs between two slices of bread rather than as a club. Get it?"

"You don't think social justice is important?"

"Well, um, *duh.*" She makes the missing-the-point gesture with her hand and fist again. "But I think your own happiness is even *more* important."

"And you don't think I'm happy?"

"I think you have most of the right ingredients in your pantry for happiness, but it's like you're using the wrong recipe."

"Okay, I'm thoroughly confused."

"I just think you're much more of a curried-lentil-soup kind of girl rather than a ho-hum sandwich. You know...bold, strong, hearty, motivating. The kind of soup that flies under the radar but is spicier than all the rest; the soup that all others are measured against."

"Huh?" I make a face.

"What's so 'huh?' about it? You're the main course, but you're so busy trying to be a side dish, you can't see the entrées through the appetizers."

I'm not so sure my "sandwich" is ho-hum, nor am I even sure what Tori's talking about. Sometimes it seems like she's speaking a language of her own. Other times, like now, though I may not totally understand her, I think the things she says sound profoundly genius.

She gets up from the chair, giving a thumbs-up to Roger's Bates Motel sign. "See you in J-Block," she tells me.

I nod, watching her clomp away in her humongous astronaut boots—like one of Waldo's clan walking across the moon.

twenty

It's after school, and Max is waiting by my locker as I come out of physics. He waves when he spots me.

"Hey," I say, dodging the mob of students en route to the exit doors.

"So, I've been thinking about the next meeting."

"*Next meeting?*" My head fuzzes.

"PB&J."

"Oh, right," I say, fumbling with my padlock.

"Yeah, I was thinking that we could join forces with one of the other similar-interest clubs on campus to boost our visibility—like the Eco Warriors for an environmental project or Amnesty International for a human rights effort."

"That actually sounds pretty genius, but I've sort of gotten involved in another project and it's taking all of my time."

"So, wait, you're abandoning ship?"

"Not abandoning ship, just chartering a boat elsewhere."

"Can't you just stay onboard with me?" He smiles. "For the next thirty minutes or so? Because I'd really love to strategize, and ultimately change your mind. I have some great ideas."

"That's really sweet of you," I say, finally getting my locker open. "But I can't today."

"So, how about Saturday, around eight?"

"You want to strategize on a Saturday night?" I swap my books for my camera and jacket.

"No." He shakes his head. "I mean, Saturday night, around eight. There's a party."

"Hannah Hennelworth's," I say, connecting the dots.

"You know her?"

"I know *of* her."

"Well, I was thinking that maybe we could go to her party together." He points back and forth between himself and me, like we're playing a game of charades. "It'd be good exposure for us—for PB&J, that is."

"*Max Terbador!*" someone shouts—a boy on the hockey team—complete with a jerking fist.

"At what age can one legally apply for a name change?" Max asks.

"I believe that would be eighteen." I grin.

"It can't come soon enough."

"Hey, guys," Jeannie says, sneaking up behind us. She's all smiles, as if someone wedged a boomerang in her mouth. "What's going on?"

"Max was just telling me about a party this Saturday."

"*Really?* Details, please," she chirps.

Her enthusiasm is mind-boggling, because super-serious/ disses-parties-in-lieu-of-extra-credit-projects/in-bed-by-ten- unless-there's-a-*Nova*-marathon *Jeannie* is not exactly the chirping type.

"Are you interested?" I ask, unable to help gawking at the pinking of her cheeks.

"Why not?" She pushes her glasses up farther on her face—a nervous tic she developed in middle school, whilst dealing with the *B*s (a group of girls whose names all began with *B* who took pleasure in making her life miserable, i.e., taping coupons for acne cream to her locker, barking in her direction, and leaving dog biscuits on her desk). The joke's on the *B*s now, however, because Jeannie is absolutely stunning—only she doesn't even know it.

"We could all go to the party," Max offers, ever the gentleman.

"Superific," she bursts.

"Great," Max says, focused on me. "I'll give you a call." He starts to walk away, accidentally colliding with Ms. Matherson, the gym teacher, as she transports an armful of Hula-Hoops to the gym.

Hoops go flying. Max scrambles to help her pick them up. Meanwhile, Jeannie and I turn away, pretending not to notice. Only once he walks away again do we burst into a fit of giggles.

"Okay, what's the deal?" I ask her. "You're totally crushing on Max, aren't you?"

"No way."

"Yes way. I mean, *seriously*? *Superific*?"

"*What?*" She shrugs. "I'm just trying to expand my social circle a bit."

"By going to some freshman wannabe's party?"

"Exactly. It's a *party*, Day, so don't overanalyze it. Just have some fun. Is that really so hard?"

I can feel the smirk on my face. I can also smell BS from a mile away. "Let's table this discussion for now, shall we?"

"Happily," she agrees, already headed down the hallway.

We move out the exit doors and around to the back of the school. The assignment for my photography class is to capture a mood, and Jeannie has insisted on coming along.

I lead her to the trail behind the field house—the one that leads to Juniper Hill. It's narrow and rocky, making me wish I'd opted for boots over ballet flats.

"Does the mood you're trying to capture have something to do with misery?" Jeannie asks, picking a cobweb out of her hair.

"Is hiking really that bad?"

"In a word: yes."

From the very peak of the hill, the ocean is like the background of a canvas. "I'm thinking of getting a shot of a lone tree, with the ocean peeking through the branches, under a late-afternoon sky."

"And what mood would that capture?"

"Good question."

"You should've taken a picture of me getting my calc test back today. It would've conveyed pure loathing. I'll bet you anything that Mr. Bedrosian has devil horns hiding in that mass of 1960s curls on his head."

"And the devil tail?"

"Down his pant leg, naturally."

"You've obviously given this a lot of thought."

The smell of burning charcoal hangs in the air, making me miss summer. We continue up the hill, finally reaching the peak. The clouds look like cotton candy that's been pulled apart and dipped into salmon-pink paint. I take a bunch of shots—some of the sky and the ocean alone, a lot more of the sky and the ocean as a backdrop to an evergreen tree.

Jeannie sits down on a rock. She takes off her glasses and closes her eyes. Her hair blows back in the breeze, away from her face. I take the shot. My shutter clicks. "Anything mood-worthy yet?"

I squat down to take her picture, able to capture the pursing of her lips and the furrowing of her brow. I scoot down even lower, stretching out on the ground, eager to get an upward angle, noticing a tear running down her cheek. She looks sad and beautiful at the same time.

I take the shot. My shutter clicks again.

Jeannie opens her eyes and glares at me. "What do you think you're doing?"

"Capturing a mood, remember?"

"And which mood do you think I am?"

"Only you can say for sure."

"Dark, frustrated, gloomy, depressed. Take your pick."

"I'll take 'Gloomy for a thousand, Alex,'" I say, trying to cheer her up by playing *Jeopardy!*

"Today's the anniversary."

I move to sit beside her, racking my brain, wondering what she's referring to. "Josh's death," I say. The answer hits me like a truck.

Josh was Jeannie's older brother. He died three years ago

while walking along the side of the road, hit by a car that had lost control during a rainstorm. It was thirty-five minutes before the Jaws of Life were able to pry him out from beneath the car. By that time he was dead.

"It's supposed to get easier, right?" she asks.

I wrap my arms around her, remembering summer four years ago, when Josh tried to teach us how to surf, and the winter after that when we all went snowboarding.

"I miss him," she says, breaking the embrace, voicing my very thoughts. "And what makes things worse...Josh was the wonder boy—good at everything, loved by everyone, turning whatever he touched into gold. And I know it sounds totally whiny—and I actually hate myself for saying it—but it's kind of hard to live in the shadow of your perfect dead brother." She looks at me again. Tears slide down her face.

My mind immediately flashes to my superhero parents. "You know, you're pretty *wonder-girl* yourself."

"Whatever." She rolls her eyes.

"I mean it. You're one of the smartest people I know, with an Aretha Franklin voice, not to mention you're stylish, beautiful, fun—"

"Even if part of me wanted to believe those things were true, my heart tells another story." She wipes her eyes with her sleeve.

"Well, then I'll keep telling your heart...until the words finally stick."

"But they'll just be words. How can I ever make myself believe them when Josh is gone, when I keep trying to live up to his memory?"

"Okay, seriously? You could become the first female president and find the cure for cancer. You could end world hunger and stop global warming . . . but that still won't change the fact that Josh is gone and that you have to go on living."

"I know." She nods. "Logically, anyway."

I wrap my arms around her again, wishing I could take my own advice about living in other people's shadows. But I haven't figured that out yet either. For now—*for her*—I'll just pretend that I have.

twenty-one

twenty-one

When I get home from school, the house is overwhelmingly desolate. I switch on some lights and click on the TV, trying to trick myself into believing that I'm not really alone. I also send out a couple of texts—one to Jeannie, including a picture of the two of us with Josh, standing at the top of Mount Snow during our ski trip. My other text is to Tori, looking for more details about the party this weekend (not that I even want to go).

I just want to feel less alone.

In the kitchen, I heat up some dinner for Julian, feeling

anxiety bubble up in my gut, unable to help thinking about that one classmate who said that Julian used to talk about getting rid of his dad.

Of course there was also the teacher who stated that Julian had a gentle soul, and the friend who said that Julian had been his first go-to. But does either of those last two testimonials help ease the wad of tension burning beneath my ribs?

Unfortunately, no.

Still, I head out to the barn with my tape recorder, my list of questions, and my cell phone and pepper spray. Julian comes to the door. The waist of his pants has been gathered on one side, the slack wrapped with a rubber band.

"Hungry?" I ask, handing him a container filled with mac 'n' cheese, along with a plastic fork.

He tears off the lid, stabs the noodles, and shovels them into his mouth as if he hasn't eaten in days.

"I probably should've brought more."

"You don't have to bring me anything at all. I'm not some caged bird that you need to feed."

The comment feels like a slap across my face, heating up my cheeks. "You're free to leave whenever you want. Caged birds can't."

"You're right. Past tense: I *was* a caged bird." He turns to clean off a couple of bales of hay and then sits down on one of them.

I sit down beside him, catching another glimpse of the pickax tattoo on his wrist. "And did that help you unlock the cage?"

He yanks down his sleeve. "It's not what you think."

"How do *you* know what I think? Are you having a bad day?"

"Every day for me is bad."

"If you want I could come back another time."

"No. It's fine." He takes a deep breath. "Let's do this."

I press the RECORD button and place the tape player between us.

ME: When you went to the beach on the weekend of May 4th and 5th, you mentioned that one of the surveillance cameras had been broken.

JULIAN: Right, one of the cameras in the parking lot.

ME: You said that the surveillance cameras picked you up on Sunday. Where did they spot you and when?

JULIAN: Coming back from my spot on the rocks.

ME: What time was that?

JULIAN: Around 4:40 maybe.

ME: Did you walk by the shower area?

JULIAN: No, I think I must've gone the other way—along the deck side, where people eat—because that's where the camera caught me.

ME: Do you always take two different routes to and from the rocks?

JULIAN: Which route I take depends on where my car is parked.

ME: Where did you park on Saturday versus Sunday?

JULIAN: On Saturday, I got a spot on the right side, by the entrance. On Sunday, I was way over on the opposite end of the lot, by the boardwalk.

ME: What time did you get to the beach on Sunday?

JULIAN: Maybe around ten or eleven in the morning.

ME: The morning after the bodies were found, correct?

JULIAN: Yes.

ME: Had the police come by then?

JULIAN: Yeah. I called them the night I found the bodies.

ME: And where did you stay that night?

JULIAN: Protective Services came for me, but since I don't have any relatives in this area, my friend Barry's mother convinced them to let me spend the night at her house. The following morning, Barry's mom made breakfast and was trying to get me to talk about stuff, but I just wanted to get away, so I went to the beach.

ME: Stuff, meaning your parents? And the details of what happened?

JULIAN: Yes.

ME: And did you talk to her about either?

JULIAN: No. I didn't want to. I was still too shocked about everything.

ME: What was your relationship like with your father?

JULIAN: Let's just say he wasn't the nicest guy to be around.

ME: Not nice because *he* . . .

JULIAN: Drank, had a temper, made my mom feel like crap most of the time.

ME: Why did he make her feel that way?

JULIAN: Because he resented her.

ME: *Because* . . .

JULIAN: It's a long story.

ME: We have plenty of time.

JULIAN: . . .

ME: Julian?

JULIAN: I used to have a brother—a twin. His name was Steven, and he died at five years old.

ME: Julian . . . I'm so sorry. I had no idea.

JULIAN: Yeah.

ME: How did he die?

JULIAN: Car accident.

ME: Did he get hit by a car?

JULIAN: No. He was in the car. I was too. Our mom was driving.

ME: And what happened?

JULIAN: She was angry. My dad hadn't come home when he said he would, so she had to bring us on her errands. The car lost control and slammed into a tree, on Steven's side.

ME: Did she hit a patch of ice?

JULIAN: No. Mostly she was just driving too fast. She'd swerved to avoid slamming into another car, but instead she slammed into a tree.

ME: Did help come right away?

JULIAN: It did. An ambulance, the police, people on the street . . . But it was all too late. Steven's death was instant.

ME: I'm so sorry.

JULIAN: I am too. It should've been me.

ME: How can you say that?

JULIAN: Steven and I'd been fighting about car seats. I liked the blue one, but he wanted it too. In the end, I won out, and Steven . . .

ME: Do you want to take a break?

JULIAN: No, it's okay.

ME: Did you and your mom get hurt?

JULIAN: Not physically.

ME: But emotionally.

JULIAN: Emotionally, everything just fell apart. I blamed myself. My parents blamed themselves. They both blamed each other for not making different choices.

ME: Do you remember what life was like *after* Steven's death—how you all dealt with the loss?

JULIAN: My mom sunk into depression and my dad started drinking.

ME: And you?

JULIAN: I cried every night. I hated myself after that. I think my dad hated me too.

ME: I can't even imagine how hard that must've been.

JULIAN: Yeah, not exactly an ideal upbringing. Aside from my friend Barry, I never had any close friends—never wanted anyone to see what was going on inside my house.

ME: I'd almost think your parents would've been *extra* protective of you after something like that happened— that they'd have been afraid of losing you too.

JULIAN: My mom shut down. Maybe she didn't want to get too close in case she somehow lost me too. My dad resented me for insisting on the blue car seat and then walking away without a scratch.

ME: How did you deal with his resentment?

JULIAN: I'm here, aren't I?

ME: Yes, but for what reason?

JULIAN: Because people think I killed my father—that I got so mad after finding my mother's body in the tub . . .

ME: Julian?

JULIAN: . . .

ME: The people that think you killed your father . . . what's their theory? How do they say the details of the crime went down?

JULIAN: Most of them think that I became so enraged, blaming my father for my mother's death—for driving her to suicide—that I killed him.

ME: What is that theory based on? Where is the proof?

JULIAN: I used to talk a lot of shit, telling friends that I *wanted* to kill him. I didn't mean any of it for real. But imagine seeing your mom so depressed all of the time. Imagine hearing your father whittle her down—until she no longer spoke above a whisper or got out of bed, until she barely weighed ninety pounds and had razor marks on her wrists. I wish I could say that I didn't hate my father. But I did. I *do*. And I'll tell anyone who asks me the same.

ME: Still, talking about killing people isn't exactly proof.

JULIAN: Having a crappy alibi doesn't help the situation.

ME: I'm almost surprised your parents didn't get a divorce.

JULIAN: Why divorce when there's so much torture to be had?

ME: You said before that you think your mother is responsible for your father's death.

JULIAN: That's right. I think she'd probably been planning it for a while.

ME: What makes you say that?

JULIAN: She hated him more than anything. She hated the way he treated us, but she was always too broken to do anything about it. So, I think that finally, yeah...this was her way of making up for lost time.

ME: And then after she supposedly killed him?

JULIAN: I think she took a shitload of pills and drowned herself in the bath. I think she...

ME: Julian? Maybe we should take a break.

I press STOP, trying to imagine what this must be like for him— having lost his parents, being accused of an unspeakable crime, unable to see his friends.... "Is there anything I can do?" I ask him.

He peeks up at me. His face is red. His eyes look swollen. "You can tell me something about you now."

"About me?" I shift uneasily against the bale. A blade of hay pokes through my jeans, into my thigh, sending a hot, prickly sensation straight down my leg. "Like what?"

"Anything."

"Okay, well, my real name is *Sandra* Day, rather than just Day. Our family name is Connor, which my parents took as an opportunity."

"To name you after a Supreme Court justice?"

"Not just *any* justice—the *first female*."

"Except your last names aren't *exactly* the same, right?"

"No." I sigh. "I'm missing the O."

"Pretty rough." He grimaces. "Missing vowels right out of the gate."

"Seriously." I smirk. "Being named after someone like that...it pretty much puts a curse on your whole life—like, there are all these expectations right out of the womb."

"Is that why you go by Day?"

I nod. "It adds a layer of distance."

"And how about all of that stuff you threw into the trash? Did it have anything to do with living up to those expectations?"

I grin, impressed that he gets it. "It was some meeting materials for a club at school—a social justice club, basically. My meager attempt to make a difference."

"Well, you've made a *big* difference to me." His gaze makes a zigzag line from my eyes to my cheeks, landing on my mouth, causing my heart to stir.

"I should probably go," I say, feeling my face flash hot.

"Yeah," he says, getting up, averting his eyes, taking a

couple of steps back. He replaces the lid on the mac 'n' cheese. "Thanks for the food and for listening to what I have to say."

I muster a polite smile, and then go for the door, part of me wanting to listen more, another part scared out of my mind that I've already heard too much, that I've gotten involved at all.

twenty-two

It's three in the morning and I've yet to fall asleep. My heart is racing. My skin won't stop sweating. The ceiling is like a giant movie screen, replaying the images inside my head: Julian and his brother in the backseat of a car; Julian crying; his mother screaming; her body floating in a tub.

It's all too much.

I'm sleeping too little.

Finally, around four, I grab a notebook and write stuff down.

FACTS SO FAR

1. It's unclear whether Mrs. Roman's death occurred before or after Mr. Roman's.

2. Her body was found in the bathtub, with the water still running, assumed to have been a suicide because she'd taken a lot of pills. (Though it's also possible her overdose could've been accidental; i.e., perhaps Mrs. Roman didn't realize how many pills she was taking.)

3. According to Julian, Mrs. Roman had suicide scars on her wrists.

4. Mr. Roman was last seen in front of his house not long before his death.

5. It didn't appear as though anyone had broken into the family home on the day of Mr. Roman's murder.

6. According to Julian, he's the one who called the police when he found the bodies.

QUESTIONS

1. Had Mr. Roman just arrived home? Or was he home already? If the first is true, why didn't he call for help when he discovered his wife's body in the tub? If the second is true, why didn't he notice the running water? Surely there must've been water spilling onto the floor, seeping beneath the door crack (unless Mr. Roman was already dead by the time the water was an issue).

2. Was Julian really at the beach the whole time this was happening?

3. How many surveillance cameras are at Dover Beach? And where are they located?

4. Is it a coincidence that Julian happened to walk by a working surveillance camera on Sunday and by an area that didn't have any camera at all on Saturday?

5. Is Julian innocent?

6. Did Mrs. Roman murder her husband and then kill herself?

7. Did this crime have any other suspects? And, if so, who were they?

I gaze toward the window, unable to stop obsessing over the timing of it all—Mr. Roman's murder occurring on the same day as his wife's alleged suicide...Why weren't investigators able to figure out the order of their deaths?

I do a quick Google search with the words "autopsy" and "time of death estimation." There are numerous sites devoted to crime-scene forensics. I click on one of them. It seems there are several factors involved in determining the time of death, including body temperature, rigor mortis, and the cessation of organs.

But what about when a body is immersed in water? According to Forensic Fred, self-proclaimed *CSI* fanatic, if the tub

water is warm it might quicken the cessation of organ func-
tion while also speeding up rigor mortis. On the flip side, if
the temperature's cold, those same reactions might be slowed
down. I'm assuming the water in the tub was warm—at least
initially, until the water in the heater emptied.

But what if it wasn't?

I get up and pace back and forth, the questions bopping
around inside my brain like an annoying pinball game. I really
need to sleep. I have a history test tomorrow.

The blare of fire trucks nearby fills the loud silence. I wonder
if Julian hears it too. I look toward the window of the barn,
willing to wager a bet, desperate to ask him the one obvious
question that's been raging inside my brain. How else will I
ever be able to get any sleep?

I woke up, all out of breath, to the screeching of sirens. It was dark out. Late night? Early morning?

I got up and stumbled across the barn, accidentally bumping into the mower, wishing I had a flashlight. I went to peek out the window and spotted Day.

She was standing in front of her bedroom window, staring in my direction. The lights were on in her room. I backed away and placed my hand over my chest, able to feel the pulsating beat.

What the hell am I doing? Why the hell am I staying? I mean, yes, I still have unfinished business, but why aren't I doing it?

Day got up and swung open the door to her room. The light downstairs flicked on. She was in the kitchen, grabbing something from behind the door. The porch light went on. The back door opened.

Standing on the porch, she clicked on her flashlight. I moved to the door, wrapped my fingers around the handle, and held my breath, fearing she was coming to see me, half-hoping she was coming to see me.

There was a light rap on the door. I edged it open.

Day was there. And I immediately got that feeling: a fluttering in my stomach, a tightening in my chest like I suddenly couldn't breathe. I took a mental step back, trying to get a grip, wondering how the hell this happened. It had to change. I needed to go.

"I couldn't sleep," she said. "Your case has been spinning around inside my head—"

"And?"

"And are you really, truly innocent?"

I closed my eyes, flashing back to being five years old, sitting on the floor of the living room—in my fuzzy red pajamas, on the dark blue rug—playing with my Matchbox cars while my father yelled at my mother in the kitchen.

"Did you do it on purpose?" he snapped at her. "Was the accident part of some scheme to get me back for coming home late? Did you even bother to check the kids' seat belts?"

Mom sunk down against the cabinets and cried like I'd never heard before—a deep-throated wail, like nothing that sounded human.

"Julian?" There was a concerned look on Day's face: parted lips, scrunched brow.

What was the question?

"Did you do it?" she asked; the very same words my father used.

I want to tell her I did. I want to make her hate me. "That's the hard part," I said, instead, "because who would ever answer yes to a crime like that? And yet, at the same time, you don't even know me. You have no real reason to believe me if I answer no."

"What if I told you that I don't care if the answer's no."

"Then *who'd* be lying?"

"Are you guilty?" she asked, for the third time.

I clenched my teeth, still able to picture my mom, the last time I saw her, lying in the bathtub with a dead stare in her eyes. "No." I shook my head.

She twitched from the cold, wrapping the coat tightly around her. "I'm trusting that's the truth."

"And I'm trusting you won't turn me in."

If only that made us even.

twenty-three

After school the following day, Tori picks up Jeannie and me, having scored her mom's car for the week.

"Is your mom feeling extra charitable or something?" Jeannie asks, peeling an ice-cream wrapper off the seat.

"No, she's just feeling extra guilty."

"Guilty *for* …" I open the window a crack. The interior smells like fuzzy cheese.

"Sucking up my life, basically." Tori puts the car in drive and pulls out of the parking lot, but instead of turning left toward home, she merges right, slamming on the accelerator.

Jeannie flips the sun visor down to gawk at me in the mirror.

Her expression—bulging eyes, raised brows—matches my thoughts exactly.

"You need to slow down," I insist.

Tori blows out a raspberry, denoting her disagreement, but thankfully she eases up on the accelerator, so that Jeannie and I can breathe. "Wouldn't it be great if we could Wite-Out entire chunks of our life?" she asks. "Like, if the liquid inside that tiny white wonder bottle could erase all of our screwups and annoyances?"

"Would that include facial protrusions?" Jeannie lifts her glasses to run her finger over the nonexistent bump on her nose.

I edge forward in my seat, placing my hand on Tori's head-rest. "What would you Wite-Out?"

"Only the fact that my mother is preggers."

Jeannie's mouth gapes open. "You're joking."

"No joke. Sixteen weeks. And here I thought Mom's recent rolls were the product of too many Mr. Goodbars."

"But instead they're the product of your dad's good bar?" Jeannie asks.

An image of Tori's dad immediately pops into my mind: beer belly, suspenders, tiny round glasses. He's basically a darker-haired version of Santa Claus; even Tori calls him that.

"Okay, um, *ew*," Jeannie says, once again reading my mind. "Are you sure she's pregnant and not just bloated?"

"Definitely sure. I found the pee stick in the garbage. Two lines, unmistakable."

"And this sucks up your life, *because* ...?" Jeannie asks.

"Because Santa isn't the father."

"Pull over," Jeannie demands.

Tori does as told, coming to a full stop at the side of the road—ironically, outside Millie's Maternity. She puts the car in park and rests her head against the steering wheel. "Do you guys remember a few weeks ago, when I went home during C-Block to get my history paper? I saw them. That is, I walked in on them...*together*."

"*Ew,*" Jeannie repeats.

"Wait, you saw *who*?" I ask.

"My mother and Hugo the electrician. Evidently he'd been coming over to screw more than just her bulbs." Tori lifts her head from the wheel. "It's like a cheesy Lifetime movie, except for the fact that I have no idea how this ends. She's keeping the baby, by the way, even though she and the baby-daddy have broken up."

"Does your dad know?" I ask.

She nods. "He knows everything—about the pregnancy and the fact that the baby isn't his."

"*And?*" I persist.

"And how does he feel about the fact that my mom was

playing hide the Mr. Goodbar with the man who lights up her life—*literally?*" Tori asks.

"Okay," I say.

"Miraculously, he's already forgiven her. And P.S., he's excited about the baby. But you know Santa. He's overly generous, always merry to trim her tree and jingle her bell."

"Okay, I'm seriously going to yack." Jeannie rolls down her window.

"Can we go get double-fudge lattes now?" Tori asks.

"We can get anything you want," Jeannie says.

"But only if you let me pay," I insist, remembering Dad's money in my wallet.

Tori gives us the thumbs-up and begins on the road again. We pass through the cities of Marshton and Wallington, finally crossing into Decker, Julian's hometown.

I already know where we're headed. Tori's favorite coffee shop is a place called the Pissy Ragdoll. Its logo is a Raggedy Ann–looking doll giving the middle finger.

We pull up in front and go inside. The place is frequented by an eclectic mix of hipsters, drama rats, emos, and artsy types. There's a huge bulletin board that takes up the wall by the pickup counter. It's littered with postcards, posters, job ads, and moody quotes. We order our drinks and gravitate to the board, per usual. Someone's posted a bunch of illustrations—ink drawings of famous couples (John Lennon and Yoko Ono, Luke Skywalker and Princess Leia, Prince William and Princess Kate).

"Ken and Barbie," Tori cheers, looking somewhat like a Barbie doll herself (or at least the superhero version of one), complete with a hot-pink bodysuit that matches her hair, white ankle boots, and shimmery gold cuff bracelets. "I wish I had my own Ken right about now."

Jeannie rolls her eyes. "You need a Ken like I need a monkey on my head."

"Actually, a monkey *could* come in handy to carry all of our drinks." Tori turns on her heel to get her Whiny Ragdoll but instead of coming back to join us, she heads in the direction of the gaggle of boys in the corner.

"So much for girl bonding," Jeannie says.

"*We* can bond," I offer.

"Over French vocab, I hope. Quiz tomorrow, remember?"

"Right." I cringe, reminded of the history test I took today. Though, on barely three hours of sleep, it actually wasn't as terrible as I thought it'd be.

While Jeannie grabs her Funkin' Ragdoll (a mint-mocha latte), I move to the far end of the bulletin board, noticing a group of kids swarming a poster.

A tall girl nods to it. "I'm surprised they're using this photo.

I mean, isn't that his yearbook picture? Shouldn't they be using a mug shot rather than a head shot?"

"Maybe that's the whole point," another girl says; she's dressed in soccer gear. "To nab our attention. Like, who's that hottie convict?" She laughs.

I peek between them. A picture of Julian's face sits beneath the word WANTED, sending a shockwave through my body.

"I can't believe he's still missing," Tall Girl says.

"*I* can," a boy pipes up; his hair is as red as the Pissy Ragdoll's. "The cops in this town are a joke. And the guards at the juvie? Useless as decaf. Isn't this, like, the third breakout this year?"

Julian looks so different in the poster. His face is fuller. His hair's much shorter. His eyes appear less tired. But still I'm able to recognize his smile: the curious grin that curls up the side of his face.

"I actually think it's the fourth breakout," Tall Girl says. "At least that's what my dad told me."

"I'm glad Julian got out," Soccer Girl says. "I mean, he never really talked much—at least not in my bio class—but he always did his work and stuff."

"He was always writing in his notebook," the red-haired boy says. "Probably plotting out his crime."

"I'll bet he was really sweet," Soccer Girl says.

"Sweet for an ax murderer maybe." A girl with jet-black

curlicues uses a plastic knife as a makeshift ax to chop through the air. "I heard he used his bare hands."

"His father suffered a blunt-force trauma to the head," a guy with a spiked faux-hawk says.

"Are you suddenly the authority on Julian's case?" Curlicue goes to take a sip of her large iced coffee, but the straw misses her mouth and shoots up her nostril.

"Wait, didn't Mrs. Roman have *some secret ex-lover?*" Soccer Girl makes her voice go sexy-sultry.

"Holy shit," Faux-hawk says, checking his watch. "I have to go."

"So do I." Soccer Girl looks up at the clock. "My shift starts in ten minutes, and I still have to change." She pulls a hat from her bag. The café's pissy ragdoll sits on the visor, giving me the finger.

The group quickly disperses, as if I suddenly smell like the inside of Tori's car.

"I guess *you* know how to clear out a room," Jeannie says, standing by my side now. She hands me my drink. "Who's the guy?"

At first I assume she's talking about Faux-hawk, but then she moves closer to the poster of Julian.

"He looks so familiar," she says. "Do we know him?"

"That's the guy," I tell her. "Julian Roman."

She angles closer to get a better look. "The bike-path-stalking-convenience-store-daddy-murderer? I totally recognize him from the news."

"*Alleged* daddy-murderer," I say, correcting her.

"Where's Tori, by the way?"

"There." I nod to the cushy chairs in the corner of the café. Tori's sitting with a couple of Jimi Hendrix look-alikes. "I guess somebody's feeling better."

"I guess somebody wants a distraction."

"Nothing wrong with that," I say, suddenly eager for a distraction too. "So, how about that French vocab?"

"Right this way, *mon amie*." Jeannie taps her Funkin' Ragdoll against my Dolly Latte and then leads me to her table.

twenty-four

Before we head back to town, I ask Tori if we can make a pit stop at Dover Beach.

"Because you're looking to freeze your ass off?" She nods to the temperature gauge on the dashboard. "It's forty-seven degrees."

"More like because I want to check out the surveillance cameras."

"Planning something shady?" She tsk-tsks. "If so, I'd pick something a little less conspicuous than a beach."

"Like a library reference room or something?" Jeannie laughs.

"It's sort of a long story," I tell them.

"And does the premise have anything to do with a certain juvenile-detention-center escapee?" Jeannie peeks at me in the visor mirror.

"Am I that transparent?"

"Like window glass." She yawns.

"It was those kids," I tell her. "In the coffee shop. They were talking about Julian's case. His alibi was a girl who originally said she saw him at Dover Beach on Saturday, but the surveillance cameras only peg him there on Sunday."

"I seriously don't even understand why you care," Jeannie says.

"Because I'm interested in his case," I remind her. Why is the idea of that such a mystery to people? "I want to make sure that his arrest was justified."

"And how do you propose to do that? Interview key players? Ask to see the surveillance tape? Take a crash course in forensics?" Jeannie snickers. "Who has that kind of time, not to mention the resources?"

"We're here," Tori declares, pulling the plug on our conversation.

The car rocks from side to side as we drive onto the gravel lot. Things look vacant without the summer traffic. Sully's Snack Bar is closed. All of the picnic tables have been put away.

"I'll just be a second." I grab my camera from my bag and

get out. The snack bar's ordering and pickup windows are boarded up for the season. A surveillance camera points down at them from the corner of the building. I take a snapshot of it, remembering how Julian mentioned bumping into Ariana by the showers.

I move around the corner. The showers are in open view, on a platform, under a wide overhang. There's no surveillance camera anywhere, but then why would there be? Who'd shower if they knew they were being videotaped?

I take photos of the shower area anyway, trying to picture what the scene looked like: Julian had just arrived after mowing his neighbor's lawn. It was around noon. He said he parked his car on the right, by the entrance, and then walked on this side of the building, which makes perfect sense. He wouldn't have walked around to the other side. This route would've been more direct.

There's another surveillance camera in the corner of the building, but it's pointed at the deck area, where people eat. I take a photo of it, figuring it must've been the camera that caught Julian on Sunday, when he parked on the opposite side of the lot.

I take photos of the beach, as well as the rocks to the far right, where Julian said he liked to sit. The rocks form a mountain of sorts—about as tall as a one-story house. There are also a few flat slabs, and a couple of alcoves where one could find shade. But there are no cameras out that way.

A flagpole sits a few yards from the deck. There's a surveillance camera attached to it. More cameras point down from poles along the boardwalk, to the left. I take photos of all of them, especially the one in the far corner of the parking lot. According to Julian, that's the camera that was broken. But why would that even have mattered for him if he'd parked by the entrance like he said on Saturday? And if the camera by the deck caught him on Sunday...

I head back to the car, my mind whirling with questions.

"You're seriously researching this case, aren't you?" Jeannie turns in her seat to gawk at me.

"Um, were you not conscious for the last twenty minutes?" Tori asks her. "I'd say the answer's a big fat yes."

"It *is* a big fat yes," I admit.

"Because you really think the police screwed up?"

"What I think is that the published details don't add up, and so I'd like to find more facts. If it ends up being a waste of my time, so be it—at least I'll know."

"It's never a waste of time if you learned something in the process," Tori preaches.

"Reading your mom's self-help books again?" I ask her.

"I know. I should stop. Those books are obviously full of crap. My mother wouldn't be boinking other guys if her life were so evolved."

Jeannie shudders once again.

twenty-five
twenty-five

It isn't until after five that Tori pulls up in front of my house, after having dropped Jeannie off at home.

I give her a hug. "Call me for anything, okay?"

"Does anything include adoption?"

"You want this new baby to be adopted?"

"No, I want *myself* to be adopted."

"By *my* parents?"

She puckers her lips in thought. "Okay, maybe not. They'll sense my mediocrity before the papers are even signed."

"Are you kidding, my parents love you": the truth. Another

truth: my mom has said on more than one occasion that Tori is very sweet, but that she's also as flighty as an airport. "Call me, okay?" I blow her a kiss and step out of the car.

As usual, the house is empty. At least when my parents were together, they made it home for dinner, but now there's really no point. I'm sixteen, old enough to eat by myself and keep busy with my studies.

In other words, I'm pointless.

In the kitchen, I load up a bag of food, wondering how long it's going to take my mom to notice that our groceries are evaporating faster than beer at a fraternity house. I also fill a box with more donation clothes and bathroom essentials. Arms full, I take everything out to the barn and rap lightly on the door.

Julian opens it up.

"Hey." I smile.

He smiles back, but I can tell he doesn't want to; I can see the resistance in the tightening of his lips.

He takes the box and peeks inside, plucking out the pair of scissors I packed. "This is very trusting of you."

"If you really wanted to hurt me, you'd have done it by now." I glance at my dad's toolboxes. They're filled with enough sharp objects to stock a hardware store.

"How do you know for sure?"

I *don't* know for sure. "Do you want this stuff or not?" I ask, pretending to be tougher than I am.

He turns away, sets the box down, and picks up the hand mirror I packed him. "Wow," he says, looking at his reflection.

"Wow... *different?*"

"Wolflike."

"I actually saw a picture of you recently, *pre*–Teen Wolf."

He looks up from the mirror. "Online?"

"On a poster, at a coffee shop in Decker—"

"The Pissy Ragdoll?"

"That's the one." I grin.

"Was the picture sitting underneath the word WANTED?"

"Being wanted isn't such a bad thing," I say, trying to be funny, but quickly realizing how wrong it sounds.

Julian nods, glancing at my mouth before turning away again.

"Some of your classmates were there," I segue. "A boy with red hair, a girl who plays soccer... There was also a really tall girl and some guy with a faux-hawk."

"And what were they saying?"

"It seems you have at least a couple of people in your corner: The girl who plays soccer and the boy with the faux-hawk... I'm pretty sure they think you're innocent."

"And the others?" Julian moves to sit on a bale of hay.

I sit down beside him and pull the tape recorder from my

pocket. "There's actually something else I wanted to talk to you about."

He looks down at the tape recorder, but he doesn't make a comment, and so I push RECORD.

ME: Someone at the coffee shop mentioned your mother might've been seeing someone else.

JULIAN: Misty said that, right?

ME: I don't know anyone's name.

JULIAN: The girl with straight dark hair, dressed in soccer gear. She also works at the coffee shop.

ME: Yes, that's the one. Why would she say that? How would she know?

JULIAN: Because Misty's friend used to ride at that guy's ranch.

ME: That guy?

JULIAN: The one my mom used to cheat with. He owns a horse ranch in Brimsfield. Their relationship happened a long time ago. I'm surprised Misty's still talking about it.

ME: How did *you* know about your mom's relationship?

JULIAN: I remember coming home and seeing a truck parked in front of our house. At first I thought it was part of a surprise for me. The sign on the door said Hayden's Horse Ranch, and I'd always wanted to try riding. I was around eight or nine at the time.

ME: But it wasn't part of a surprise...

JULIAN: My mom and that guy were kissing inside the truck. They didn't see me coming.

ME: How long did their relationship last?

JULIAN: Not long—maybe a couple of months.

ME: How do you know it didn't last longer than that?

JULIAN: That's what my mother told me.

ME: Did your dad know about the relationship?

JULIAN: No.

ME: So it's possible that your mom and this guy could've still been seeing each other.

JULIAN: I doubt it.

ME: But it's possible

JULIAN: . . .

ME: Was he questioned at all—this ranch guy, I mean?

JULIAN: I don't know.

ME: Did the police ever talk to you about him?

JULIAN: No.

I press STOP. "You need a good lawyer—someone who's going to ask these questions and interview the right people."

"No lawyer would be able to help me unless I turned myself in."

"Maybe that's not such a bad idea."

"I thought *you* wanted to help me."

"I do. It's just . . . this is way too important to screw up."

"So don't screw up."

"No pressure or anything." I take a deep breath and let it filter out slowly. "Can you talk about your grand plan?"

"My *grand plan*?" His face is a giant question mark.

"You escaped from juvie, laid low, found my barn, and got sick. But then what?"

"Then I met you."

"But what if you hadn't? What were you planning to do? Where were you planning to go?"

He bites his lip, mulling the question over. Is it possible that he had no plan—that he was just taking things day by day? Was the juvenile detention center really that awful?

"If I'm going to help you, you have to be honest with me—about your planning and your parents, about what happened at home, and everything that's going on in your brain."

He's not even looking at me now. He's angled away, facing the wall. I reach out to touch his forearm, and suddenly everything else stops: my babbling, his lip-chewing, the sound of hammering outside . . .

Julian's eyes lock on my hand. "This is all kind of new to me." His voice is fragile—like it could shatter with just the right words.

"What is?"

He pulls his arm away, putting an invisible wall between us. "You really need to go." He gets up and goes for the door.

"Tell me first."

"*Go!*" he shouts.

His tone cuts through my core. A chill runs down my spine.

I get up and wrap my hand around the pepper spray in my pocket. "You don't scare me," I lie.

His hand balls into a fist, like he wants to strike out. "You *should* be scared. You should go home and forget you ever met me."

I move closer, just a few feet from him now. "I already am home. This is *my* barn. And I don't have to go anywhere."

He opens the door a crack, as if about to leave, then shuts it instead and turns to face me. His jaw is stiff. His eyes look red.

I position my finger over the nozzle of the pepper spray, just in case. "You won't hurt me," I say, nodding to his fists; both of them are clenched now.

"How do you know?"

"Because you're not a monster."

"*How do you know?*"

I take a step closer, feeling my insides shake. He's shaking too. Maybe it's because he's holding himself back. Or could it rather be that he's just as scared as I am?

"Don't you have anything better to do?" he asks, after several moments.

"Like what?"

"Like being with your boyfriend."

I maintain a poker face, wondering why he's asking. Could it possibly be that he saw me with Max? My gut reaction is to correct him, but I keep silent instead, because he doesn't need to know.

"What did you mean before," I ask, "when you said that this is all kind of new to you?"

"I meant this. You. *Us*. Talking to each other, that is." He peers over his shoulder, as if there's anything there to look at besides a stone-cold wall. "Aside from my one friend, I never really told anybody anything. I just wrote stuff down."

"Journals are great"—I take another step—"but they can't replace real people, real relationships . . . those we can trust."

"They can when there's so much to hide." His gaze roams all around the room—at the toolboxes, the mowers, the ceiling, and Dad's golf stuff—except at me.

"I really want to help you," I say, eager for him to hear the words again, to know he has someone in his corner—for now at least, until I have reason not to be.

Day put her hand on my forearm, and I don't know what it was, but I totally lost my shit. My head went spinny and my heart started to race like I'd just run a marathon. I bolted for the door, but I couldn't bring myself to go, and she wouldn't leave.

Finally, I searched the room for something to distract myself, digging back into the box she brought. I took out a comb. I hadn't seen one in weeks.

"I thought you might want to spruce up a bit," Day said. "I mean, no big deal—just if you want..."

I attempted to run the comb through my hair—to show her I was so far beyond sprucing. As expected, it got stuck.

"I actually have a trick for that." Day grabbed a jar from the box. The next thing I knew, she was sitting me down, standing behind me, spreading peanut butter on my hair.

"You really don't have to do this."

She maneuvered the comb free, then unscrewed the cap to one of my water bottles. Water spilled over my head like a baptism. She washed my hair next. The shampoo smelled like strawberries and felt like an egg yolk. She massaged it through, scrubbing every inch of my scalp.

"I can probably handle things from here," I said, feeling ridiculously self-conscious.

She rinsed my hair again, and then started to comb it once more. This time it worked. No knots. Smooth sailing. She grabbed the pair of scissors. "Would you like a cut too?"

I knew that she should go, and part of me really wanted her to. But another part would've sat for an entire head shave if it meant spending more time with her. I watched as chunks of my hair fell to the floor.

"This is going to be great," she said, angling the scissors around my ears and clipping strands from in front of my eyes.

Several minutes later, she scooted down in front of me. Sitting between my knees, she pulled at the ends of my hair, checking to make sure that the length was even. In doing so, she accidentally bumped her hip against my leg, sending a wave of heat straight down my thigh.

"Can you imagine?" She laughed. "A lopsided frizzball… It was pretty hilarious."

I pretended to be listening—to know what she was talking

about—but she lost me at the thigh bump. "Pretty funny," I said, trying to play along, unable to help staring at her lips. They were so completely distracting: the color of dark roses. The corners of her mouth turned upward as she pushed back my layers.

"So, do you?" she asked.

I opened my mouth to answer, but no words came out, because I didn't know which ones to use—words to describe a bad haircut I once got, or to explain why I had no idea what she was asking me.

She continued to pick at my hair, moving strands forward and back, like I had anyplace to go.

"I'm sure it's fine," I told her.

Her fingers slid down the sides of my face. It was almost too much to handle—her attention, her touch.

I wanted to stand up. I should've moved away. What the hell was I still doing here?

"Never trust a woman," my father used to tell me. "They'll mess with your head and take everything that's yours, including your every thought."

Her fingers stopped at the cut below my eye. "Where did you get this?" she asked.

"When I left the detention center."

"When you escaped," she said to clarify, not letting me forget: I didn't just leave. I wasn't simply released.

"When I escaped." I nodded. There was so much I wanted

to tell her—*so much she didn't know.* "My face met a jagged piece of metal fencing."

"Lucky that it didn't meet your eye." *She sat back on her heels. There was a weird expression on her face, like she was suddenly confused about something.*

"For the record, I don't really care if you screwed up my hair."

"It's just that you look really different."

"Different good?"

"Different different." *There was something else on her mind.* "Here," *she said, forcing the mirror into my hands.*

I peeked at my reflection, less than interested in my hair. I would've given almost anything to read her thoughts or to kiss those dark rose lips. "It's great," *I said, noticing that it looked a lot like it had before my arrest—shaggy, just an inch or so past my ears, longish layers, and waved to the side.* "Do you do this for a living?"

"If I did, I'd have to charge you." *She got up from the floor. She smelled like the shampoo—like something I wanted to bottle up and wash all over me.* "So, do you think you could give me some names?"

"Names?" *I asked.*

"Yeah. The names of the people I should talk to about your case, or a list of the things you'd like me to check out. Think of me as your very own private investigator."

"Except once you start asking questions and probing into the case, people will find out who you are. And then figure out where I am."

"Not if we're smart about it." She looked at me, waiting for a response, so excited about the prospect of helping me and saving the day.

I wanted to believe she could. But instead my dad's words continued to play in my mind's ear: "Don't trust 'em for a second. They'll promise you the moon, stab you in the back, and leave you more alone than ever."

twenty-six

In my room, I curl up on my bed with a slice of blueberry pie, eager to feed this ache: this stirring sensation inside my heart, the weight of Julian's loneliness on top of my own. In one way, I wish I'd never even started this investigation—this view into a world that's so much darker than my own—but in another way, I wish I were back inside the barn, holding Julian's hand, and giving him back a bit of light.

I grab my phone, seeking some sort of connection, noticing a missed call from Max. I dial Tori instead.

"Forgot to ask," she says, in lieu of hello, "did you manage to score any numbers this afternoon? I was so focused on my own score sheet that I lost track of you and Jeannie."

"As if the Pissy Ragdoll is a score-sheet kind of place."

"Did I not spot you in a swarm of hunky hotness sipping something tall, dark, and delicious?"

"Um, *huh*?"

"I scored two numbers, for the record, thanks for asking."

I take another bite. "I was only eavesdropping on the swarm. I kind of wish now that I'd actually talked to it...*them*."

"Which has got to be one of the most overrated of pastimes, if you ask me—talking, that is."

"Maybe if our parents did more talking, there'd be less family drama going on."

"And maybe if our parents did *less* talking, there'd be more lusting going on."

"Okay, that's gross."

"You're right, but I'm feeling a little bit better about things, FYI. Of course, the guys at the coffee shop helped. Bojo told me that he has six half siblings he's yet to meet—and those are just the ones he knows about."

"Bojo?"

"Remember this: Bojo equals boho."

"As in, from Bohemia?"

"As in free-thinking, unconventional, totally nonconforming."

I look at the receiver, suddenly wishing I'd called Jeannie instead. "Have you tried talking to your mom?" I ask, in an attempt to switch gears.

"Talking, overrated, remember? Though there was one thing that Bojo said that really hit home: the choices our parents make—that we all make, for that matter—have a distinct purpose that may not seem apparent on the surface."

"For the record, my head is officially spinning."

"This is Life School," she says. "And there are specific lessons we need to learn in this lifetime. And so we choose different paths, based on how we respond to those lessons, thus creating our own unique consequences."

"Are you sure Bojo didn't slip you a special brownie with that double-fudge latte?"

"My mother's decision to cheat on my dad is part of her journey," she says, ignoring me. "Hers, Santa's, the electrical baby-daddy's . . . and mine as well."

"How is it part of *your* journey?"

"That's the best part, because I don't know yet. It'll be one of my many life's missions to figure it all out."

I lean back in bed, almost jealous of her newfound perspective—even though I don't quite get it. "You sound so evolved."

"Bojo is ah-maze," she says. "I just spent the last two hours on the phone with him."

"Even though talking is overrated?"

"I'm just *so* glad I met him," she says, ignoring the comment. "And *see*: our choice to go to the coffee shop after school...it was meant to be, because I met him."

And I got to eavesdrop on some of Julian's classmates.

"Bojo's father is the minister at this new-age ministry in Glenville," she says. "He invited me to an ice cream social Saturday night. I know what you're thinking. It sounds totally blue-haired-ladies-in-a-church-basement-playing-bingo-and-eating-sour-cream-and-onion-dip, right? But Bojo promises it'll be epic."

"And what about Hannah Hennelworth's 'It's-Saturday-let's-party' party, aka Operation Make Jarrod Koutsalakis Jealous?"

Tori lets out a sigh. "And how do you suppose I make him jealous if he's already taking someone else?"

As if the operation was my idea.

"Am I supposed to dress like a ho and flirt with every guy in his path?" she continues.

"Wasn't that the plan?"

"You really think I'm that shallow?"

I look at my phone, wondering if I'm on some hidden camera show, or if she's taping this conversation as a joke.

"Whatever, it doesn't matter." She lets out another sigh. "I no longer have time for cat-and-mouse games. What I need is a man who'll help me grow into a better person."

"Like Bojo."

"You totally get me, don't you?" I can hear the smile in her voice. "Not many people get me, you know."

"Go figure." I stuff my mouth with more pie.

I ran from juvie without ever looking back, cutting through the woods behind the facility, swiping branches and brush from in front of my eyes.

A road was coming up. I could hear the swish of cars.

I tripped over a low branch, falling on my face. Blood ran from my nose. A stick stabbed into my neck.

Swish. Swish. *Two cars whisked by. I got up, my back aching, and I continued to move forward, stopping just a few yards from the road. All was quiet. I crept a little closer. Three more cars went by before there was an empty road.*

I raced across, spotting a strip mall in the distance. Half of it looked abandoned. The other half consisted of a drugstore, a liquor store, and a twenty-four-hour market. There were two cars in the parking lot. It didn't appear that anyone was in them.

The facility's siren screeched. I could feel it in my bones. Standing in open view, I didn't know what to do. Cross the street again? Go back into the woods? I looked at the strip of stores and then at the parked cars. Did I still remember how to hot-wire? But both cars looked too new for hot-wiring.

Beyond the strip was another road. No houses. Not much traffic.

The door of the liquor store swung open. I hurried behind the strip before the person saw me, spotting a Dumpster.

I climbed inside without looking down, landing on a pile of bags—wet, plastic, shit-smelling, stomach-turning. Something stung my face. I touched the spot. Blood came away on my hand.

Broken glass. An old wine bottle.

Police sirens blared. I moved into the corner, burying myself with crap—boxes and bags and old, half-eaten food—flashing back to the day we buried Steven. In the cemetery, Mom was sitting in a chair. There weren't many people. My parents liked to keep things private—just a couple of cousins I'd never met and an aunt who lived 2,000 miles away.

Dad didn't cry. He stood off to the side, watching as the casket was lowered into the ground. He hadn't spoken in days except to say that since Steven could no longer speak, we shouldn't either.

I wanted to cry. But I wanted to be like Dad even more,

and so I sucked in my tears and bit my shaking lip, watching as the priest sprinkled holy water.

"He's buried now," Mom said later. "All gone."

I remember thinking that I liked to bury things too: string beans in my mashed potatoes, candy wrappers between the sofa cushions. Though those things never really went away.

And neither did Steven.

twenty-seven

There are more than fifty photos loaded up on my computer screen, old photos that I worked so hard to get, that capture vivid colors and/or play with things like natural and artificial light or macro-filters for magnification. They're all so perfectly staged: the product of countless hours spent planning how I'd wanted things to look.

But what do they really say? They don't show anything real. They only give the illusion of reality, which somehow feels dishonest.

I start to dump them into a folder labeled "Make Believe," just as the phone rings. It's Max.

"Hey," I answer.

"What are you up to?"

"Trying to get inspired, but failing miserably."

"Sounds like someone could use a little caffeinated motivation. Can I bring you a coffee from Java, the Hut?"

I look at the clock. It's just after seven. Should I let him?

"It's not that hard of a question," he says.

I wish that it weren't.

"Or is it?" he asks.

"How about a rain check?"

"Sure. Consider me your caffeine source."

"I'll remember that." I smile, really wishing this weren't so hard. I hate that I'm disappointing him. But I hate, even more, that we can't be friends rather than awkward acquaintances.

I hang up and take a snapshot of myself: I'm the picture of confusion. But still, as confused as I am, I'm suddenly feeling inspired. I pocket my tape recorder, run downstairs to grab the keys to Dad's old clunker (or, as he likes to call it, his priceless antique Scout), and pull out of the driveway.

The roads are quiet tonight, but Dad's antique is not. It rumbles every time I step on the accelerator and stalls when I hit the break.

I reach the Pissy Ragdoll in twenty-five minutes flat. Misty, aka Soccer Girl, is still here, cleaning one of the coffee machines.

My pulse quickens as I approach the front counter. Her back

is to me as she continues to clean: *wipe, wipe, spray, repeat.* I push RECORD on the tape player and clear my throat.

"Can I help you?" She tosses her rag into the sink.

I look up at the menu, wondering if I should order something.

She turns to face me. "Hey, do I know you?"

"I was in here earlier," I say, glancing back at the poster of Julian on the wall. "And I heard you talking about Julian Roman."

Her expression shifts from neutral to annoyed in under a blink. *"And?"*

"And I'm a student at the university. We have a class called Crime and Caseload, where we delve into local and semi-local cases to pick them apart. My group is researching Julian's case."

An older guy—the manager maybe—passes behind her to fiddle with the espresso machine. Misty grabs another rag and pretends to wipe the counter. Meanwhile, the guy pours himself a fresh cup of coffee and moves out of eyeshot.

"To be honest, I don't really know Julian that well," she tells me.

"Okay, but do you think I could ask you a couple of questions anyway? I really need to do well on this project. I bombed the first assignment, and he gives us credit for effort."

She studies my face before peering over at some guy stocking the shelves. "Tag, can you cover for me?"

Tag nods, and Misty leads us to a table by the window. We take a seat, opposite each other.

"His case doesn't exactly look too good, does it?" she says.

"What makes you say that?"

"Well, the fact that he got arrested is a big tip-off. Word also has it that he hated his dad. Plus, his alibi didn't check out. And it seems there was so much he lied about."

"Like what?"

"Well, the lawn-mowing gig, for starters. He said he mowed the neighbors' lawn in the morning, but the owner of the house swears it was more like three in the afternoon, when Julian was supposed to be at the beach. And speaking of the beach... he claims he was there all day, but the cameras didn't catch him, even though it seems they caught everybody else. Then he said he came straight home to find the crime scene, but he wasn't wearing beach clothes. He was still dressed from mowing the lawn."

"I think I read somewhere that he didn't go to the beach to sit out or swim. It was May anyway—probably too cool for either. I heard he liked to sit, write, and read," I say.

"Still, wouldn't you change after mowing a lawn? Especially if you planned on spending the entire day at the beach?"

Honestly, I don't know.

"And then I heard that Julian went out somewhere after

coming home from the beach...but I'm not sure if that was before or after his parents were found dead. I don't know." She shrugs. "It's all so confusing."

She's right. It is.

"What was your name, by the way?" she asks.

"Day," I say, but just as soon as I say it, I wish I could take it back.

"*Day?* Weird." She laughs. "Not that 'Misty' is totally normal. Anyway, the other sticky piece in all this is that the cameras *did* place Julian at the beach on Sunday, the day after his parents both died, and if that's true, it's seriously messed up. I mean, who goes to the beach after that?"

"You don't think his mom could've done it?"

"Sure I do. I mean, that's the logical choice. Even though I didn't know him well, I've been going to school with Julian since kindergarten, and it seems that things in that family have gone from bad to worse. Mrs. Roman went from showing up at pickup and walking Julian home from school to hiding in her parked car and then to not showing up at all."

"Did you know Julian's brother?"

Her eyes widen with surprise. "Julian Roman had a brother?"

"Forget it." I wipe the words away by swatting through the air. "Why do you think Mrs. Roman got progressively worse over the years?"

Misty shrugs again. "People say that she was hard-core depressed—like in-need-of-a-warning-label depressed: Keep all sharp objects away."

"Is it true that she was seeing someone else?"

"I heard that too. And I think she probably was—the guy who owns the horse ranch in Brimsfield—but it had to have ended years ago. I mean, seriously?" She rolls her eyes toward the ceiling. "You don't even understand: The woman was a walking zombie. I bumped into her once at the supermarket; it was like the *Night of the Living Dead* buys a loaf of bread and a pound of cheese. I can't even imagine what she was like at home."

"Did anyone ever question the guy from the horse ranch?"

"*What*, am I FBI?"

"Misty?" Tag says, nodding toward the clock.

"I have to go. I still have a shitload to do before closing time." She stands from the table.

"One last question: Do you know how I can reach Ariana, the girl from the beach? Or that guy with the faux-hawk?"

"Barry," she says, correcting me. "You should definitely talk to him. He was, like, Julian's one and only. I think he'd love the idea of a college doing research on Julian's case."

"Misty?" the manager calls.

Misty takes out her phone. "What's your number? I'll share

Ariana's contact info with you—she won't care. But Barry? I can see him getting all moody about it unless it's on his terms, you know. I could have him text you."

"Great." I rattle off my number.

"Good luck with your assignment."

"Thank you. So much." I stand from the table.

"And, hey, if you learn anything scandalous, you know where to find me." She turns away just as my cell phone vibrates with her text.

twenty-eight
twenty-eight

I round the corner of my street. My house is still dark. No one's home. I pull into the driveway, pressing the trigger that opens the garage, noticing a car parked in front of my house. Not either of my parents'.

A Jeep. Olive green. The light clicks on inside it, just as the door swings open.

Max steps out. And I don't know what it is. The deserted house? The empty sensation I feel after dipping deeper into Julian's world? Or just seeing Max's familiar face (a reminder of my own world)? But I couldn't be happier to find him here.

I lock the Scout away in the garage and begin walking toward him.

"Cool wheels."

"My dad's. He'd die if he knew I took it out."

"Don't tell me you went on an emergency coffee run without me."

My heart instantly clenches. "Were you following me?"

"Following you? No. That would make me a creep." He hands me an iced coffee; it's the perfect shade of mocha-brown. "I thought I'd surprise you. That's a medium brew, by the way, with two splashes of almond milk and a packet and a half of sugar."

"You remembered," I say, flashing back to last spring, when he took my order on a coffee run during finals week. "Thank you."

"No problem." He smiles.

I take a sip, trying to hold it all together—the details of Julian's case, the homework I've yet to finish, this paranoia I'm experiencing.

"Is everything okay?"

I can feel the emotion on my face, spreading like a fever across my cheeks. "Do you want to sit for a minute?"

"Definitely."

We take a seat on the front steps. The chilly autumn air blows against my skin, making me shiver—and the icy coffee isn't helping. "Have you ever felt as though you're in way over your head?" I ask him.

"Pretty much on a daily basis," he jokes. "Are we talking about the PB&J club?"

"A PB&J-club type of situation—well, kind of. In the same stratosphere, maybe."

"That sounds pretty clear." He smirks.

I know. It doesn't. "Let's just say that I'm trying to solve the situation single-handedly, and I'm feeling completely overwhelmed."

"Why? I'm happy to help." He bumps his shoulder against mine, causing the ice in my cup to rustle.

"I know."

"Then what?"

I stare downward, at my shoes. My fingertips are turning numb. "I really want to help this person, and part of me thought I could, but now I'm not so sure."

"Wait, you're not talking about that case again, are you? The guy from juvie?"

I press my eyes shut, feeling my insides cringe.

"Holy crap, you are."

"I just thought that I could help him."

"Help him *what*? You haven't talked to the guy, have you? Do you know where he is?"

"No," I lie. "It's just . . . we're talking about someone's entire future here. I wanted to make sure that his arrest was warranted, because from everything I've read, it seems he's being used as a scapegoat."

"Wow."

"*Wow*, I'm totally crazy?"

"*Wow*, you're pretty incredible."

I shake my head, holding back tears. "I'm not. Really. I actually feel like I'm failing him."

"Even though you don't even know the guy?"

I hold in a breath, wondering how well I *do* know Julian.

"Well, honestly?" he continues. "If I were in that sort of dire situation, with my future depending on it, you'd be the person I'd want in my corner."

"For real?" I look up from my shoes.

"No doubt."

"You're really sweet, you know that?" I say, noticing once again how blue his eyes are—the color of sea glass.

"I'm not trying to be sweet. Ever since I've known you—"

"Since kindergarten," I remind him.

"Right, since kindergarten . . . you've always stood behind whatever you felt passionate about. Remember, in second grade, when Ms. Meany wanted us to collect caterpillars so that we could research their life cycles? You wrote a letter of complaint to PETA. None of us even knew what PETA was.

Then, in sixth grade, you stood before the school committee asking if you could help raise money for healthier food initiatives, including educating the nutritional staff on the harmful effects of food additives, pesticides, and TMOs."

"GMOs," I correct him.

"No one knew what you were talking about."

"And so they did nothing, including Ms. Meany, who ended up with five sacrificial caterpillars because, let's face it, re-creating the natural conditions of a monarch takes a whole lot more than branches, grass, and an overhead light."

"See that?"

"*What?*" I sigh, feeling more defeated by the moment.

"You fight for what you think is right."

Correction: I've fought for what I thought would make my parents proud. "And you can see how far my fighting has gotten me."

"Probably a lot further than you think. Who knows what kind of ripple effect you've caused—all the people who've watched, and listened, and admired you over the years. Like me."

"Well, thanks," I say, thinking how everything he's saying...it's sort of how I've always felt about my parents, but never about myself.

"If there's anything I can do—with this situation or anything else—to help you, remember, I'm always here." He flashes me a shy smile.

I smile back, wishing I could be the person he thinks I am: the superheroic woman I've always aspired to be.

What would that feel like?

Even for just a moment?

He looks back up, and I venture to touch his hand.

"Day?" His face furrows in confusion.

I lean in closer and kiss his questions away. His fingers tangle up with mine as he pulls me toward him. I can sense how into the moment he is—much more of a kiss than I anticipated.

And still I don't feel superheroic at all.

I pull away, and our lips make an unpleasant sucking sound. "I'm really sorry," I tell him.

"Don't apologize," he says, running his hand along my forearm. His touch fills me with guilt, because I know he doesn't get it. And because I know that's my fault.

"I should probably go inside," I say, hating the sound of my voice. "I still have a bunch of homework."

His eyes remain locked on mine, probably trying to figure me out. Sandra Day Connor: the Queen of Mixed Messages. Finally, when he sees I really mean it, he backs away slightly, letting go of my forearm. "Sure." He tries to smile, but I can see the disappointment on his face, wriggled across his lips.

"But I'll see you tomorrow, okay?" I say, as if that's supposed to make everything better.

We stand from the steps. Max waits until I get the door

unlocked and open—until I've inserted, turned, and extracted the key; twisted the knob; and pushed the door wide.

"Good night," I say.

There are so many questions on his parted lips, but he doesn't speak one of them, which somehow makes things worse.

I watch him walk away, toward his car. The night sky swallows him up. It also creeps inside my heart and tears a gaping hole.

I remember it was scorching out that day, because I was bare-foot in the driveway, and the hot-top burned the bottoms of my feet. I could hear the cartoon show inside the house. Little Ferngrow's Garden—*the part where the snail sings the song about moss.*

I was five years old.

"Go stand in the grass where it's cool," Mom said.

We'd been locked out of the house. I wasn't sure why, but I suspected it had something to do with Steven.

"Come on, Juju," Mom said, taking my hand and bringing me into the backyard. "I want to show you something." She grabbed a couple of shovels from my sandbox, along with a few pieces of colored chalk.

She led me to the picnic table and crawled beneath it. She started to dig a hole.

"Help me out here, will you?" she asked.

I joined her under the table and dug in with a shovel, happy to be playing this game with her. I loved my mother more than anything.

She fished one of Dad's handkerchiefs from her pocket, and with the chalk, wrote a word across the fabric. "See that," she said, pointing to it. "It's the word PAIN. The p makes the puh sound, a-i makes ay, and the n sounds like nnn. Pain."

"Pain," I repeated. "Are you in pain?" I asked her.

Her eyes looked sad. "If we bury our pain, we can make it go away." She dropped the handkerchief into the hole.

"Just like we buried Steven."

"That's right," she said. "We can bury anything we like. Pretty neat, huh?" She smiled. "Now, it's your turn. What would you like to bury?"

I wanted to bury Steven's bed and storybooks. I thought that if they went away, maybe we could go back to the way things were before. But things never went back, no matter how much I buried.

I started to distrust my mother then. She didn't protect me. She hadn't protected Steven. And she never protected herself. What kind of a mother is that?

twenty-nine

In my room, I grab my phone and look for Misty's text, eager to distract myself from the fact that Max and I kissed.

Our lips mashed.

Our tongues touched.

I close my eyes, able to picture the confusion on his face, almost unable to believe that it happened.

But it did.

And I did it.

I push RECORD on the tape player, set my phone to speaker mode, and press Ariana's number. The phone rings, and suddenly I realize that I have no idea what I'll say to her.

ARIANA: Who's this?

ME: Is this Ariana?

ARIANA: It is, and *who's this?*

ME: I'm a student at Crest Hill State University.

ARIANA: Oh, right. Misty texted that you might call me.

ME: Is it okay if I ask you some questions about Julian Roman's case?

ARIANA: For the record, I'm *not* friends with Julian, so I have no reason to try and cover for him or anything.

ME: Cover for him?

ARIANA: Like when I told the police that I saw him at the beach on Saturday rather than Sunday. To be honest, it was weird to even be talking to Julian Roman. He'd never said a word to me prior to that day.

ME: Do people think that you were lying about the day?

ARIANA: Apparently some people do.

ME: So, was it Saturday or Sunday?

ARIANA: That's obviously the problem. I mean, I originally thought it was Saturday. But when I really stopped to think about it, I was at the beach on both days. I remember because I was participating in this volleyball tournament thing that weekend. Anyway, when the police told me they caught Julian on surveillance video on Sunday, rather than Saturday, and then when they asked me if I was a hundred percent sure about the date, I couldn't help but second-guess myself. I mean, could it have been Sunday?

ME: I guess that's a good question.

ARIANA: I know, right?

ME: Why did you originally think it was Saturday?

ARIANA: Because I had a soccer game that day. I vaguely remember him asking me about it. I think we might've even laughed over the fact that I'd headed my soccer cleat—by accident, mind you—during the second half of the game.

ME: Did you tell that to the police?

ARIANA: I did, but then they kind of messed me all up, pointing out that we could've been talking about the soccer match from the day before. I couldn't really argue. I mean, my mind was scrambled. My heart was racing hard-core. I seriously hate talking to cops. But wait, I thought the whole alibi-at-the-beach thing wasn't even relevant anymore.

ME: Why wouldn't it be relevant?

ARIANA: Because when Julian came home from the beach, his father was still alive.

ME: Wait, *what*?

ARIANA: You don't know?

ME: Know what?

ARIANA: Okay, so I don't have all the details, but apparently a UPS guy delivered a package to the Romans' house sometime after Julian had gotten home from the beach that day. The guy overheard Julian and Mr. Roman fighting, and so he peeked into the window.

ME: And what did he see?

ARIANA: Julian and his dad, in the living room. I guess the fight was pretty loud. The UPS guy confirmed it happened on Saturday, by the way.

ME: So then Julian lied about coming home from the beach and finding his parents dead?

ARIANA: Who knows. I mean, maybe he lied. Or maybe, like me, he got mixed up, too. Let's face it: police aren't exactly the easiest people to talk to.

ME: How come I'm just hearing about this UPS guy now? Why wasn't he in any of the news reports?

ARIANA: Well, for one, I guess the guy came forward really late, which is why I initially got raked over the coals about when and where I saw Julian at the beach. And, for another, I don't think news reports disclose everything. I mean, right?

ME: Do *you* think Julian did it?

ARIANA: I don't know. He never struck me as the killing type. But then again, like I said, I barely knew the guy.

ME: I really appreciate your talking to me.

ARIANA: So cool that your group is researching the case.
You have my number if you think of anything else.

I press STOP, suddenly realizing that, like Misty, Ariana has my number now too.

thirty

"We need to talk." It's after nine when I push past Julian into the barn.

"Did something happen?" he asks.

I turn to face him, noticing right away: smooth tan skin and chiseled jawline.

He shaved his face.

And changed his clothes.

Wearing a pair of jeans that hug his thighs, and a blue waffle shirt that clings to his chest, he looks undeniably beautiful.

I look away, trying to stay focused. "I read something," I utter. "A news report. It said that a UPS guy spotted you and your father fighting after you got home from the beach that day."

"That's right," he says, without the slightest flinch.

"So then you *didn't* come home to find the bodies."

"I did. It's just…" He moves to sit down on a bale of hay. "I was so screwed up after coming home and finding them, I didn't think to mention going out for a drive in between. And then, when I did think to mention it, it was way too late."

"Hold on," I say, pulling the tape recorder from my pocket. I sit down beside him and push RECORD.

ME: What do you mean "it was too late"?

JULIAN: I mean, I was too scared to correct myself, and so I just stuck to my original story.

ME: We need to back up. What time did you get home from the beach?

JULIAN: Probably around five.

ME: And what happened once you got there?

JULIAN: My dad and I got into a heated argument that ended up getting physical.

ME: What were you fighting about?"

JULIAN: I don't know.

ME: You don't remember?

JULIAN: What difference does it make?

ME: It could make a big difference in the scheme of things—what you and your dad were fighting about shortly before his death. . . .

JULIAN: . . .

ME: Okay, so you got into an argument that became physical. What happened after that?

JULIAN: I took off before things got *really* ugly. About an hour later, I came back. That's when I found his body—in the middle of the living room floor.

ME: Where did you go when you took off?

JULIAN: I went by Barry's house. No one was home, and so I just ended up driving around.

ME: Where was your mother during the fighting?

JULIAN: Honestly, I don't know. She didn't come out.

ME: Did you hear the bathtub water running?

JULIAN: Not that I can remember. I'm thinking she must've been asleep in her room.

ME: And she wouldn't have heard the fighting?

JULIAN: Not if she'd taken some of her sleeping pills.

ME: Is there a chance she wasn't home?

JULIAN: That would've been highly unlikely for her. She was almost always home.

ME: In which room were you and your father fighting?

JULIAN: It started in the kitchen and ended in the living room.

ME: Is the bathroom visible from both of those rooms?

JULIAN: Yes. It's a small house, but we keep the bathroom door closed for the most part.

ME: So, you came home from the beach, got into a fight with your dad, took off, returned an hour later, and found your father dead.

JULIAN: I found them both dead.

ME: And what did you do then?

JULIAN: I called the police. They came. I told them what happened, but I left out the part about the fighting.

ME: Intentionally?

JULIAN: No. To be honest, I was lucky to form sentences, never mind explain precisely the way things had played out. Days later, the story was out there, that I'd come home from the beach and found my parents dead. I didn't want to correct the story at that point. I didn't think I needed to either. I mean, what was the point? I wasn't guilty. But then that UPS guy came forward, and suddenly it looked like I'd lied.

ME: How come you never mentioned any of this when we were talking about your beach alibi?

JULIAN: ...

ME: Lying by omission is still lying. Didn't you think I'd eventually find out?

JULIAN: ...

I press STOP and get up from the bale. "You lied to me."

"That's right. I did." He stares straight into my eyes. There isn't a hint of remorse on his face. "You should tell me to go."

"Is that what you really want?"

He stands, towering over me. "I lied to you. I've been accused of a heinous crime. How many more red flags do you need?"

"That doesn't answer my question." I turn away and go for the door.

At the same moment the words "please don't go" float in the air.

I stop, my hand wrapped around the door handle. "What did you say?" I swivel to face him.

"I said 'please just go.'"

My jaw tenses. "You're lying again."

"So, what are you going to do about it?"

I open the door a crack, able to feel him coming closer: a hot, tingly sensation that spreads like fire across my skin. The smell of burning leaves fills the dank space. "I really need some air."

"Nobody's stopping you."

I swallow hard, spotting his lip quiver. "Do you want to come too?"

"Is that what *you* want?"

I nod and exit the barn. Julian follows me.

thirty-one

I lead Julian through the yard, toward the wooded conservation land that borders our property. With the town's permission, my dad made a path that cuts through the land and extends to a clearing. "Just stay on the wooden planks," I tell him, wishing I had a flashlight. Still, I know these woods by heart—every tree, rock, bough, and shrub.

With each step, it gets colder, darker, the moon blocked out by the tops of trees. I swipe a tangle of brush from in front of my eyes, able to hear Julian behind me—the snapping of twigs beneath his step, the sound of his breath blowing through the air.

My mind starts to wander, thinking how far we're getting

from the house, remembering how the cell reception can be patchy in these woods.

Could I call someone if I needed to?

If I screamed, would anyone hear me?

I reach into my pocket for my phone. It slips from my grip and tumbles to the ground. I scurry to find it. Julian crouches down beside me. Together, we sift through fallen leaves and broken tree limbs, until Julian finally plucks the phone from a heap.

"Thank you," I say, taking it from his hand. His skin is rough and calloused. I imagine how it'd feel against my palm. "Maybe this wasn't such a good idea."

His forehead furrows. He looks surprised and disappointed at once.

My mouth trembles open, but I don't know what to say or how to explain this uneasiness I feel.

"You're right." He turns away so I can't see his face. "This wasn't the smartest."

I check my phone screen. There are still two bars. "No," I say, on second thought. "Let's keep going. There's something I want to show you." I begin on the path again, using my flashlight app to pave the way.

After a couple more minutes of walking, we reach a clearing with boulders set up in a circle. There's a fire pit in the center, dug into the earth, with rocks all around it.

I take a seat on one of the boulders. "Come on," I tell him, switching off the flashlight app and pointing up at the sky. "The moon followed us here." It shines directly over us like a spotlight of sorts.

Julian sits beside me.

"My dad created this space," I say. "We used to come up here as a family—like our own personal campground. We'd toast marshmallows and tell ghost stories or sing songs."

"Used to? Not anymore?"

"It's probably been a couple of years, sort of a reflection of how distant we've all become."

"Not toasting marshmallows at the fire pit hardly constitutes a family in distress."

"You're right," I say, feeling stupid for bringing it up. "It's just they're separated now. I kind of wish I'd seen it coming."

"I watched my parents' dysfunction for years and it didn't make me any better off."

"Were things always tough at home? Were there ever happy times?"

"Not after Steven's death."

I venture to touch his forearm, wishing I had something inspiring to say. But the truth is that I don't. I have nothing to compare. And I don't want to pretend I do.

"Sometimes I think that maybe Steven was the lucky one."

"Don't say that."

"It's true though. Maybe my father wouldn't have been so angry. Maybe my mom wouldn't have sunk into depression."

"And maybe it wouldn't have made a difference at all, at least not as far as your parents were concerned."

"But, for *me*. I wouldn't have felt the loss of Steven or the guilt of living. Or had to have put up with years of my parents' bullshit."

"Yes, but you also wouldn't be here right now," I say, thinking out loud, trying my hardest to understand.

"You're right. And being here is actually the only good that's come from all of this."

I look up at his face, checking to see if I heard him right, but he's staring off into space. "How come you didn't tell me that when you came home from the beach that day your father was still alive?"

"Because I really wanted your help, and I was afraid that if you knew I screwed up my original story, you wouldn't believe me about anything."

"What else are you keeping from me?"

"Just one thing: I meant what I said before. You should forget you ever met me."

"If you really feel that way, then why don't you leave?"

He swallows hard; I watch the motion in his neck. Finally, he meets my eyes again. "Because I can't bring myself to go."

I slide my hand down his arm and cradle my fingers around his palm, able to feel his warm, rough skin. Julian rubs his thumb along my wrist, and I can't help but wonder, how many nerve endings are in the hand? Five hundred? A thousand?

It's as if I can feel every last one.

We remain like this—holding hands—for several seconds without uttering a single sound. I gaze up at the sky. It's the perfect shade of midnight blue. There's a perfect number of stars in the sky. Everything about this moment feels perfectly amazing.

Except this is only the illusion of perfection.

Julian is on the run.

We have so much work to do.

I steal my hand away, putting an end to the moment. Julian responds by grabbing a long stick and poking at the fire pit, moving the brush around inside, as if there's an actual fire burning.

I look at his hand, wanting to touch it once again, imagining sitting on the boulder just in front of him, with my back pressed against his chest, and his breath heating the nape of my neck, while a fire crackles before us.

"Everything okay?" He's staring right at me.

My face is absolutely blazing. I look away, trying to refocus, and press the record button on the tape player in my pocket.

ME: I read that there was some confusion about when you mowed your neighbor's lawn.

JULIAN: The neighbors say I did it in the afternoon on Saturday, but they weren't even home that day. They'd left the keys to the shed in the mailbox, as usual. I mowed the lawn in the morning.

ME: And you were still wearing your mowing clothes at the time the police arrived to the crime scene.

JULIAN: Yes, and they were drenched at that point, from lifting my mother's body out of the tub.

ME: You mentioned before that the fight with your dad started out verbal but ended up physical. Was that the norm for you two?

JULIAN: No.

ME: So, what *was* the norm for you and your dad?

JULIAN: ...

ME: *Julian?*

JULIAN: My father and I went our separate ways, for the most part.

ME: Can you look at me and say that?

I press PAUSE. Still Julian doesn't move; he just keeps jabbing the stick at nothing.

"*Look at me,*" I insist.

Finally he does. His eyes look broken, as if they could drown me in just one blink.

"I'm on your side as long as you're being honest with me."

"You just don't get it, do you?"

"No, I don't. Because you won't tell me."

He looks away again. "What do you want to know?"

"How is it for you . . . no longer having your parents around, I mean?"

"It's surreal," he whispers. "Like a nightmare that I can never wake up from. I wish I'd done more to protect my mom. Maybe then she'd still be alive."

"You can't blame yourself for your mother's death."

"Why can't I?" He shrugs. "I do it all the time."

"Do you feel she protected you?" I ask, fully aware the question's loaded.

But this time Julian doesn't deny the fact that he needed

protection—that he and his father didn't simply go their separate ways.

"We used to bury stuff," he mutters. "My mom and I."

"What stuff? Bury it where?"

"My mom used to say that if we buried the stuff we didn't like—the stuff we wanted to go away—it would just disappear, the way Steven had. And so we'd crawl underneath the picnic table and bury all of our demons—symbols of the things that we wanted to go away. We'd bury them like a corpse."

"What were the things you buried?"

"Steven. I buried him more times than I'd like to admit. There must be at least a hundred slips of paper in the ground with his name, not to mention things of his that I was able to sneak away without my dad noticing: storybooks, race cars, mittens, a shoe. But still his memory never faded."

"And how did that affect you?"

"I could never live up to the person Steven would've been— could never do as well in school or at sports. I wasn't nearly as good-looking. I didn't run as fast, didn't speak as well."

"And all of this was according to your dad?"

He shrugs again. A stray tear rolls down his cheek. "After a while, I started to believe it too."

"Even though it's crazy. I mean, who knows what kind of person Steven would've become. And as for burying your problems... it doesn't work. They'll just show up someplace else."

"I know, but when I was younger I didn't. That's probably when my hope died."

I reach out to touch his arm, running my fingers over the pickax tattoo, noticing the goose bumps on his skin. "Is this to dig a hole—to bury what bothers you?"

He looks into my face; his eyes are raw and red. "You're the only one who knows," he says, in a voice that's just as broken.

"I really wish I'd known you back then."

"We should probably head back." Julian pulls away and continues to pick, prod, and poke at the invisible fire.

I scoot in closer and take his hand again, forcing him to drop the stick, able to feel him trembling against my touch.

"You don't know what you're doing," he says.

"I do." I weave my fingers through his, able to feel that charging sensation again, pulsing through my veins, sending tingles all over my skin. "You don't have to bury your pain anymore. You can tell it to me or whisper it to the stars."

Julian looks up at the sky, perhaps making a wish on a star. I hope that's what he's doing for real. I hope I've given him a reason to be optimistic, because, aside from love, I can't think of anything better.

Mom and I were at the park, sitting side by side on the swings. I tried to keep the same pace as her, but she kept making her swing go twisty.

"Come on, Juju!" She leaned back, let her feet shoot up in the air. "Look at me!" she squealed. Her head tilted back. Her hair reached the ground.

I flipped my legs up, but not like her. They didn't touch the chain. Mom rolled backward, fell to the ground. A stick punctured her forehead.

"Are you okay?" I hopped off my swing.

"Whoa," she said, looking out into space. Blood ran from her cut, but she didn't seem in pain. She touched her forehead. Her thumbs pressed against her temples; her hands reminded me of bird wings: frail, white, fluttering.

"Can we go home?" I asked her.

She looked at me, taking a moment to focus. The pills she'd started taking made it hard. They stole her away, brought her into a fog. I imagined that I looked cloudy.

"We're not going home yet," she said. Her eyes were full of bloody vessels—"from lack of sleep," she told me.

"Jackson's grandma died," I said. "He went to her funeral. Are we going to have a funeral for Steven?"

"We already buried Steven. He went bye-bye into the ground, remember?"

"But everyone just went home after that. There wasn't a party to say good-bye."

"Daddy and Mommy didn't want a party for our son's death. Daddy will be leaving for work in a half hour. We can go home then. But for now, let's just play." She got up. Her skirt was covered in leaves. The ends of her hair were dirty. She ran straight for the monkey bars.

I followed after her, more confused than ever. Jackson had said that funerals were for saying good-bye. I wanted to say good-bye to Steven, more than I wanted presents on my birthday or Christmas to ever come again, because I thought that maybe that was the missing key, the reason Steven still had such a heavy presence in our house. Even though we'd buried him in the ground the year before, we'd never officially said good-bye. It was as if his corpse had somehow come home with us, filling our days with nothing but sadness, guilt, anger, and blame.

thirty-two

When I get back to the house, Mom is pacing the kitchen floor with her phone clenched in her hand.

"Hey," I say, shutting the door behind me, already able to sense the tension in the air.

"Where were you?" Her tone is sharp. "I've been texting you for the last hour."

I reach into my pocket for my phone, noticing the missed messages.

"A friend needed my help."

Her eyebrow shoots up, accusingly. "What friend? Tori? Jeannie?"

"A new friend."

Mom turns her back to go into the cupboard. I wonder if she notices how suddenly bare it is. "Hungry?" she asks, grabbing a couple boxes of cereal.

"Starving, actually."

She plucks the milk from the fridge and then sets us up at the kitchen table with bowls and spoons. I take a seat and pour myself some Alphabet Crunch.

Mom sits down across from me. "Is this new friend a boy?"

I add some milk to my bowl. "It's no one that you know. Just someone who needs my help."

"That's not exactly clear."

I know. It isn't. But, "I can't really talk about it."

Mom looks toward the door, the light just dawning on both of us. "Why did you come in through the back? You didn't walk home, did you? At this time of night?"

I stir my bowl of cereal, trying to spell the word *screwed* with the cinnamon letters.

"Day?" Her eyes are wide, like fishbowls.

"I wouldn't have walked in the dark, especially not by myself. You've raised a smart girl. You have to trust me on that."

"You didn't use the bike path at this time of night, did you?"

I shake my head, almost able to see the wheels turning inside her head as she tries to figure things out—why I'm out so late, who this friend might be, why I came in through the back if I supposedly didn't walk. "Someone's in trouble," I say. "And they're trusting me with their problems—really personal stuff—so I really can't say anything about it."

She looks toward the window. I pray that Julian doesn't come out of the barn.

"Trouble, as in physical trouble?" she asks. "Is this person in an abusive situation?"

"Not anymore."

"I see." She chews her bottom lip, the wheels still turning.

"I could have lied," I remind her. "But I figured that you, of all people, would understand. I mean, you help people all the time and don't say much about it."

"Because sometimes I *can't* say much about it. Sometimes there are confidentialities that I need to uphold."

"Exactly, so you understand."

"Are *you* in trouble?"

"No." I take a bite.

"Are you sure? Would you even tell me?"

"I told you this, didn't I?"

She stirs her cereal, continuing to study my face. "The police were only recently here," she reminds me. "There's a boy on the loose."

"I know that."

"Do you? He's been accused of murdering his father."

"But maybe he isn't guilty. Maybe that's why he escaped from juvie."

"Could be, or he could've escaped juvie because he *is* guilty, and because he knew he'd be convicted at a trial."

"Okay, why are we talking about this boy?" I grin.

"*You* tell *me*." She stares at me—hard—without a single blink.

I shrug in lieu of answering, feeling my face burn, unsure what she's thinking. But I can tell she's unsure too.

"Well, I don't want you walking around by yourself at night," she continues. "I need to know where you are. And you shouldn't be out past nine without my permission."

I hold back from reminding her that she's not exactly available to ever give me that permission.

"You should've texted me," she says, as though reading my mind.

"You're right. I should've. I'm sorry I made you worry."

The tension in her face finally lifts. "Is there anything that I can do to help your friend, or to help *you* help your friend?"

"Not at this point."

"But you'll let me know..."

"I will," I promise.

She continues to stare at me, as if there's writing all over my face.

I shift uneasily in my seat, trying to maintain a neutral expression. "Is something wrong?"

Her bowl of cereal is full; she's yet to take a bite. "I'm just really proud of you," she says.

The words hover in the air before finally landing on my head and seeping into my brain. "Really?" I ask, completely befuddled.

"Really." She smiles.

"Well, thanks." I say, thinking about the irony. After all my years of trying, it took something like this—something I truly care about—to finally get her attention. And, for once, I wasn't even trying at all.

thirty-three

At school the following day, I make a beeline for Max's home-room, hoping to catch him before class. He's sitting at his desk, positioned away from the door. I go inside and sneak up behind him, noticing he's working on something for French.

"What's this?" I ask, going for humor over melodrama. "Did someone not get to finish all of his homework last night? Too busy delivering iced coffee to under-caffeinated damsels?"

"I'm pretty busy," he says, refusing to look up from his notes.

"I'm really sorry about last night," I tell him.

"It was no big deal."

"Well, to me it was." I sit down in the seat in front of him. "It's just . . . you were being so nice to me, telling me what a difference I make. I kind of just wanted to feel like that person."

"And you thought that kissing me could help?"

"I know. It was stupid."

Max looks up at me finally. "I'm busy," he says again. His face is stern, like he really wants me to go.

The response slices through my heart. I leave the room, feeling even worse than just moments ago—and so much worse than last night.

Later, at lunch, I tell Tori and Jeannie about the kiss: "I totally regret it," I say, focusing on Jeannie, suspecting how she feels about him.

"Wait," Tori says, dropping her fork mid-bite; a splattering of tomato sauce lands on the table with a splat. "You and Max Terbador exchanged actual tongue spit."

"Can we please refrain from using his full name while I'm trying to eat?" Jeannie asks.

"We did," I say, to answer Tori's question.

"*And?*" Tori asks, her eyes gaping wide.

"And I feel terrible now," I say, still angled at Jeannie. "I mean, Max has got to be one of the sweetest guys I know."

"And you just stomped on his heart." Tori tsk-tsks.

"Thanks. I feel so much better now." I feed my funk with a bite of brownie.

"How was the kiss, at least?" Tori asks. "On a scale of one to thigh-quivering, that is."

"Honestly, maybe a three." I grimace. "But it wasn't his fault. There just wasn't any spark."

"Well, then why did you kiss him in the first place?" Jeannie bites.

"Part temporary insanity?" I tell her. "Another part curiosity?"

"A third part general horniness?" Tori laughs.

I roll my eyes. "The kiss had nothing to do with being horny."

"Maybe that's your problem." Tori points at me with her fork.

"Okay, so I still don't get why you kissed him," Jeannie says.

"Is it terrible to say that maybe part of me *wanted* to feel something?"

"Which part?" Tori winks, revealing an orange-and-yellow striped eyelid that matches her scarf.

I'm tempted to ask who her look du jour is inspired by, especially since she's also wearing a navy-blue jumpsuit and a super-high faux-ponytail (that matches her pink hair). She looks a little like Belda Bubble from the Cartoon Channel, a superhero girl who fights crime with her bubblegum.

"That's not what I mean." I sigh.

"What were the two of you even doing together in the first

place?" Jeannie asks. "And what activities and/or dialogue transpired *pre*-kiss?"

"It's a really long story," I tell them.

"Well, I'm all ears," Jeannie insists, leaning in to listen better.

"Okay, but I need a little longer than just the six minutes left before the bell rings." I nod to the clock on the wall. "For now, let's just say that I've been on a bit of an emotional rollercoaster—"

"And so you decided to take a ride on the Max Terbador?" Tori proceeds to do the Cabbage Patch (the seated version of it, anyway), complete with circling hips and an arm motion that always reminds me of caldron-stirring.

"Again"—Jeannie snaps—"with his full name. And, wait, does this recent lapse in judgment mean that Max *won't* be taking us to the party on Saturday?"

"Honestly, I don't know." I take another bite of brownie.

"I really wanted to go," Jeannie says.

"Because partying it up on a Saturday night is so up your academic alley." Tori feeds a forkful of ziti into her mouth. "Will you be squishing it in before or after your six-hour study session at the university library? Or perhaps between the library and your volunteer shift teaching refugees how to read?"

"For your information, I no longer volunteer at Power to Read," Jeannie says. "I'm at the soup kitchen now."

"Right." Tori rolls her eyes. "Your lecture on diversifying the college portfolio must've somehow slipped my mind."

"Going to parties is also diverse," Jeannie argues. "Who wants a girl that's all work and no play?"

"You could play with me on Saturday night," Tori offers. "I'm going to Bojo's church social. The theme is forgiveness, and it's BYOCF&S (Bring Your Own Comfort Food and Slippers). Want to come?"

"Is that a rhetorical question?" Jeannie asks.

"I'm not so sure that Max wants anything to do with me right now," I tell her, "but I'm sure he'd still be happy to take you to the party."

"Which is what you'd secretly prefer anyway, am I right?" Tori snatches a Bugle from Jeannie's bag and gives her a knowing look.

Jeannie's face turns as red as my raspberry Jell-O. "How many times do I need to say it? I do *not* have a crush on Max Terbador."

"Would you mind refraining from using Max's full name at the lunch table?" Tori mocks her. "I'm trying to properly digest my food."

I give Tori a high five, after which the bell rings and both Jeannie and I are saved.

thirty-four

After school, I sit outside by the Eco Warriors' memorial garden and check my phone for messages, hoping to find one from Julian's friend Barry.

Instead there's a voice mail from my dad. "Hey, there," he says. "Any chance you could stop by my new place on Friday? It's on your way home from school, 33 Macomber Avenue, right across from the post office. I have the day off, so I'll definitely be home. Hope to see you. Bye."

I click off the phone and swallow down his words. They taste like battery acid and burn a hole in my gut. I hate that home for him is anyplace other than with Mom and me.

"Hey," Jeannie says, suddenly appearing out of nowhere. She takes a seat beside me on the bench. "Sorry if I was being kind of weird at lunch, about that Max stuff, I mean."

"Are you kidding? *I'm* the one who should apologize."

She shrugs, but she doesn't deny it. "So, what's up?"

"My dad. He wants to show me his new place. I guess it's really happening."

"And the 'it' in that statement would be..."

"Permanent separation, imminent divorce."

"Well, there's a sobering thought. Of course, there's no point in hitting fast-forward. Let the movie of your life play out on its own."

"Okay, you're starting to sound like Tori."

"Guilty." She raises her hand. "I stole that line from her. Scary?"

"A little."

"Okay, but stolen lines aside, maybe your dad and you will have an even better relationship now that he has his own place. That happens, you know. In the book I'm reading, Charlotte and her mother couldn't even stand to be in the same room together without throwing sharp objects at each other, but after Charlotte moved out, the two were like best friends."

"Except my parents and I already *were* like best friends. Ugh," I grunt. "I can't even stand listening to myself anymore. Seriously, how do you do it?"

"Earplugs," she jokes.

"I really wouldn't blame you." It feels bratty complaining about my parents' problems after hearing about Julian's upbringing.

Jeannie gazes out at the stretch of lawn in front of the school—all the fallen leaves. "I feel like everything's changing."

"That's because it is."

"Including Josh's death."

I look over at the maple tree, planted in Josh's memory. It's about three feet tall now. "Color me confused," I try to joke. "But last I checked, death was a permanent condition. Curable only by reincarnation."

"Okay, so maybe the memory of his death, then. It feels different now that I'm the same age that he was when he died. I can't stop thinking about that—about how he never got to go to prom, or graduate, or even get his driver's license, and how I'm getting to do all of the above. In some way, I feel like I'll be doing those things for both of us now."

"Which may seem sad on the surface, but in another way it's kind of amazing. I mean, if you're crossing these milestones for the two of you, it's almost as if he's still right by your side."

"I'd like to do something in his memory," she says. "Like maybe set up a scholarship or something. Remember how much he loved track? Maybe I could organize a marathon. People could pay to run a certain number of miles, and all proceeds would go to a scholarship fund."

"I think that's a great idea."

"I just want to do something more meaningful...not that working at the soup kitchen or any of my other volunteer pursuits aren't. It's sort of hard to explain."

"I get it. It's like that for me too—with the whole PB&J thing. It's not that the mission wasn't needed or worthwhile, it's just—I don't know—not what I'm feeling driven by at the moment. I guess when I really think about it, none of my past projects have been about passion. They've always been the product of brainstorms I've had: causes I thought might impress my parents or help me make my mark. That probably sounds pretty selfish, right?"

"It actually sounds pretty deep."

"And my name isn't even Bojo," I joke.

"You and I are so much alike." She smiles. "While you play superhero to try to impress your parents, I play it to try to get into the Ivy League."

"Okay, well, I'm done trying to impress my parents."

"And how's that mentality working for you so far?"

"Actually"—I smirk—"I've never felt more confused in all my life."

"Well, I'm glad I'm not the only one."

"It's just one of the many things we have in common, along with our mutual interest in Max." I give her a pointed look. "And before you try denying it *yet again,* I've seen the way you light up at the mere mentioning of his name—his first name, anyway." I laugh. "You're like my great-grandma's birthday cake with all ninety-seven candles."

"Okay, but you're the one that Max is crushing on."

"Crush-*smush.* If Max is half the guy I think he is, he'd be an idiot not to see what an amazing person you are."

"So does this mean you wouldn't be terribly upset if I still wanted to go to the party with him on Saturday?"

"I'd only be upset if you didn't go because of me."

"Well, thanks," she says, giving me a hug.

It feels really good to hold her like this and to have this chat—so much so that the thought of visiting my dad at his new bachelor pad almost seems like a fun idea.

Almost.

thirty-five

I knock lightly before edging the barn door open. Julian's sitting in the corner, writing in his journal.

"Mind a little company?" I ask.

He flips his notebook shut, and I sit down on the floor beside him. He smells like strawberry soap.

"Writing anything good?" I glance at his notebook cover, wishing I could read the pages inside.

"Depends what you consider *good*."

"Something funny or insightful?" The key to breaking this case, perhaps.

"I mostly like to write about stuff that's already happened. It helps me understand it more."

"I do the same thing—not with writing but with pictures." I pull my laptop out of my bag and go into my virtual gallery. I show him a bunch of stills I've done—of seashells, beach rocks, willow trees, and birds—before revealing my latest album. "I haven't given the project a title yet, but I have eight pairs of photos so far." I arrange them on the screen starting with a snapshot of a woman I spotted at the bus stop months ago. She's wearing a short sequined skirt paired with a white tank and stiletto heels. From the back it looks like she might be a model in the midst of a fashion shoot. But in the next photo, from the front, she's at least eight months pregnant. "I thought it was interesting." I shrug. "That moment of sur-prise . . . just not what you're expecting. And this one's my favorite." I point to a picture of a father and son holding hands on a walk. It's a sweet shot on the surface, but a close-up of the boy in the very next photo shows the tears running down his face.

"These are pretty amazing," Julian says, pointing to my pho-tos of the beach. One of them depicts a pretty ocean scene. The other shows that same scene but with a wider angle, capturing a trail of strewn trash. "What's your inspiration?"

"For as long as I can remember, my parents have taught me to look at life from different angles before forming opinions or making big decisions. And so that's what I've always done. Taken pictures, that is—snapshots of the things that I don't understand completely in an effort to gain perspective."

Julian looks up from the screen. "That actually explains a lot."

"Does it?" I ask, staring at the dimple in his chin.

"You look at me through your camera lens—you're even using it now—but you don't pass judgment. You just keep searching for the best angle, going in for close-ups, retreating back to get a broader view, making sure you don't miss anything."

"Am I missing anything now?"

"Do *you* think you are?"

"I'd really like to get to know you better—more about your family, what you write about in that notebook, what you want out of life."

"I think that last part is pretty shot, don't you?"

"You have to have faith."

"Faith that one day I won't have to run?"

"Faith that one day your life will be everything you dreamed."

"See, that..." He smirks. "That's the difference with you. You think I have possibilities."

"You do," I tell him. "You still have choices and a long life to live."

He smiles, seemingly amused by my optimism. "Maybe I've just never been brave enough to dream."

"News flash: it doesn't take bravery to dream."

"It does if you know you'll wind up disappointed in the end."

I reach out to touch his hand. "Then I guess I'm asking you to be brave."

His fingers weave through mine, sending heat all over my skin. He moves our clasped hands against his chest, over his heart. I can feel the rapid beat.

"I suppose you have more questions to ask." He lets go of my hand, erecting his invisible wall.

I take a deck of cards from my pocket. I was going to give it to him for solitaire, but instead I slide the cards out of the box and begin shuffling them. "Do you know how to play gin?"

"Hell, yeah." He smiles.

We spend the next hour or so playing round after round of cards and laughing at stupid jokes. If I didn't know better, I'd swear he were a boy from school, hanging out at my house after a full day of classes.

But instead I do know better.

And that's the hardest part.

In one way, I feel so grateful for bumping into Day at that convenience store, following her home, and getting sick inside her barn. But in another way, I feel so much lonelier knowing that people like her exist and that I found out way too late.

thirty-six

It's barely four thirty when my phone vibrates with a text. It's Mom, telling me she won't be home for another few hours. I grab my laptop and do a search for Hayden's Horse Ranch, checking the hours. It doesn't close until eight.

Tape recorder in my pocket, I scurry downstairs and grab the keys to Dad's Scout, hoping he doesn't take note of the mileage. About an hour later, I pull onto the ranch's street, passing by a pumpkin patch and a giant corn maze. I turn into the drive and roll down the window. The air smells sweet— like apple pie and maple sugar. Over the years, I've had friends who've taken riding lessons or gone to summer camp here, but I've never visited myself. The grounds of Hayden's Horse Ranch couldn't be more beautiful. There's a giant arena with wide-open doors, and an outdoor corral where horses roam.

I park the car and get out. A sign points me to the office. I go inside. There's a woman sitting at the front desk. She's older, sixties maybe, with a long silver braid that hangs over her shoulder.

She pauses from a Sudoku puzzle to look up at me. "Can I help you?"

I push the record button. "I'm interested in taking some riding lessons."

"Well, you've certainly come to the right place." A necklace of strung horse-shaped beads hangs around her neck. "Have you ever taken lessons before?"

"No." I shake my head. "And I'd really like to take them with the owner. I heard he's really good."

"The owner here doesn't actually *give* riding lessons."

"Really?" I cock my head, feigning confusion. "I'm pretty sure the person I spoke with said she took lessons from him."

"What was the person's name?"

"Jennifer Roman."

The woman's eyebrows shoot upward in response.

"Do you know her?" I ask.

"I do, but Jennifer Roman didn't come here for any lessons."

"Really?"

"She and the owner knew each other pretty well, if you catch my drift." She winks. "But that was years ago."

"How many years?"

"Oh, I don't know." She glances back down at her puzzle. "Four? Five? Must be around there, because we now have a four-year-old horse we call J.R." She nods toward a side window. There are stables just beyond it.

"Wait, J.R. for Jennifer Roman?"

"Are you interested in taking lessons with anyone else?" she asks, forgoing an answer.

"I guess I'm just really confused. Do you think I could meet the owner anyway?"

"I'm pretty sure he's left for the day." She pulls at her horse necklace and makes a clicking sound with her tongue. "But let me check. Can you hold on for a few minutes?"

"Sure." I nod.

The woman exits the office, and meanwhile I head for the doorway behind the front counter. I move down the hallway, checking all the rooms: a bathroom, a sitting area, a kitchen, and an office.

I step inside the office. There's a desk littered with all sorts of files and equestrian magazines. A calendar hangs behind the desk. It's covered with marked dates for appointments, horse shows, meetings, programs. I flip back to May 4. The words DAY OFF are scribbled across it. I pull my cell phone out of my pocket and take a snapshot of the date, just as a thwacking sound startles me.

I freeze in place. My chest instantly tightens.

But the noise is outside—the sound of wood against wood, like the opening and closing of a gate.

I let out a breath and open the top drawer of the desk. It's full of junk, including random toys: a Slinky, a yo-yo, Silly Putty eggs, and a few mismatched dice cubes. I close the drawer and open another one; it's a file cabinet, loaded with folders. I do a quick scan, spotting a tab labeled "receipts." I pluck the folder out and go to peek inside it, just as I notice something else.

On the desk.

A picture of a pony.

I pick up the frame and turn it over in my hands.

"Peter?" a male voice shouts.

I dart out from around the desk, tucking myself behind the door.

The picture frame is still in my hands. The folder's tucked under my arm. The calendar's still set for May.

"Pete?" the person asks. He's standing in the doorway now. I can see him through the crack below the hinge.

I hold my breath, trying to keep from making a sound, but then my stomach growls and I'm sure he can hear it.

"Hello?" he asks, taking a step inside the doorway.

Part of me is tempted to come out, but not two seconds later, he turns away; I hear his footsteps move down the hall.

With trembling fingers, I open the back of the picture frame, thinking how I sometimes like to tuck notes or letters behind key photos. I don't get the latches undone on the first try. The cardboard's too thick. I have to pry upward on the latch with my thumb.

That works.

The latch slides open.

I do the same with the other latches. They open as well. I remove the cardboard backing. There's something hidden behind the horse photo. I take it out—a four-by-six photo of a woman, mid-laugh.

She's pretty, with dark hair, green eyes, and a heart-shaped face. I go to take a photo of the picture just as the file folder slips from under my arm. Receipts scatter onto the floor. They're everywhere—by the door, under the desk, in the far corner.

I scurry to pick them up, on my hands and knees.

The main door opens. I can see it from where I'm standing. The woman from the desk is back.

"Hello?" she shouts.

My heart pounds. My skin starts to sweat. I still need a picture of the photo. With trembling fingers, I take the shot.

Something falls; there's a loud clank sound; it came from another room.

I return the photo behind the pony picture, place the cardboard back, then fasten all the latches.

I go to set the photo where I found it on the desk, but it topples over, against the wood, making a knocking sound that echoes inside my bones. Footsteps move across the floor— heavy boots, wooden heels.

I turn to look.

No one's there.

My pulse racing, I put the frame back before gathering up the remainder of the receipts. I stuff them into my bag, along with the folder. There's no time to return things inside the desk.

I move out into the hallway. The woman's positioned away from me.

"Thank you," I say. I'm all out of breath. "I found the restroom."

The woman looks me up and down, as if trying to figure me out. "Peter's already gone for the day."

"Okay, well, maybe I'll come back on Saturday to see him. Does he work on Saturdays? Or maybe he's only here on some Saturdays," I say, suddenly remembering that I never fixed the calendar in his office.

"He works. On Saturdays." She goes back to her Sudoku cells, clearly done with me.

"Well, thanks," I say, still puzzled as to why he took off Saturday, May 4.

Coincidence? Or something more?

thirty-seven

At home, I park Dad's car back in the garage and head straight for the barn.

"Hey." Julian smiles as soon as I come through the door.

"I have something I want to show you," I blurt, plucking my cell phone out of my pocket. I find the snapshot I took of the woman's photograph. "Does this person look familiar to you?" I ask, angling the screen so he can see it.

Julian takes my phone and turns away. "Where did you get this?"

"It was a photo that I found. I took a picture of it."

"*Where* did you find it?"

I move to stand in front of him. "Tell me who it is first."

"It's my mother. Now, where did you find it?"

I nod to the bales of hay, and we sit down beside each other. I tell him about my visit to Hayden's Ranch, including about the calendar and the pony named after his mom. "I really think this might be a major break for us. I mean, if they were seeing each other even *four* years ago...that's a lot more recent than the seven or eight you mentioned before."

But Julian appears less than convinced. He takes a deep breath and lets it filter out slowly. "It was a long time ago."

"But not as long as you thought. Right?"

He gives me back my phone. His mouth is a straight tense line. I thought he'd be more excited.

I look at the picture of his mom—her smiling face, the brightness in her eyes. "Is it hard seeing your mother this happy?"

"Only because she was capable of such happiness, and because I didn't get to see it much. Life would've been a lot different if I had."

I stare toward the side of his face, trying to imagine what this must be like for him, learning that his mom might've had this whole other secret life. "It must be weird to think about her being with someone else."

"I think 'sad' is a better word."

"Sad because she was cheating on your father?"

"No, sad because she kept that happiness from me—because she didn't take me to the place where happiness existed."

"Maybe she was too scared to take you there."

"Too scared, too selfish, too weak. Take your pick. Which would be the most acceptable?"

"I'm really sorry."

He nods. His chin quivers. "In some way, even though I was little, I kind of knew how she felt about that guy. I saw how happy she was when she got out of the truck that day. But I guess I didn't realize it was—"

"Pony-naming serious?"

"Yeah." He bites his lip—to stop the trembling maybe—and gazes at my mouth.

I venture to reach into my pocket for the tape player, thinking about all the info I've already missed. "Is this okay?"

Julian turns away in response. His whole body stiffens. Recording these sessions puts a definite wedge between us. But I push RECORD anyway.

ME: Do you have any idea why your mother and Peter Hayden might've broken up?

JULIAN: Her depression might've been a motivating factor; either that or the fact that she was married, or her fondness for prescription meds. Once again, take your pick.

ME: Do you think it was your mom who broke off the relationship, or Hayden?

JULIAN: I'm assuming it was my mom. She'd never leave my dad, even if she did love someone else.

ME: What makes you say that?

JULIAN: Well, for one thing, she never *did* leave my father. I also don't think she wanted to leave me . . . even though, in reality, she was never really there for me after Steven's death.

ME: She could've taken you with her.

JULIAN: I really wish she had.

ME: Why do you think she didn't?

JULIAN: Because my father made her feel worthless, and deep down—even though it probably sounds nuts—I think that's how she wanted to feel.

ME: You think your mother wanted to feel worthless?

JULIAN: I think that's all she felt she deserved after what happened to Steven.

ME: She looks so happy in the photo. Do you remember her like this?

JULIAN: I remember her being like that *before* Steven's death.

ME: Not after?

JULIAN: Only a handful of times, maybe. But then she'd walk into my room and see Steven's bed, and that would be the end of that. I remember in a couple of instances Dad giving her crap about smiling too big or laughing too hard. As soon as you crossed the threshold of our house, it was like walking into a morgue.

ME: I'm almost surprised she ever came home at all.

JULIAN: You really think this is smart: going to Hayden's Ranch, asking suspicious questions, and rifling through someone's office?

I push STOP. "No one suspected anything."

"How do you know?"

"You're going to have to trust me."

Julian gets up and runs his fingers through his hair in frustration. "Maybe this was a big mistake."

"Which part?"

"This, me, staying here."

"You can leave anytime you want," I remind him.

"Is that what *you* want?" He turns to face me again. His golden-brown eyes fix on mine.

"No." My face heats up. "I'd really like to help you. But if I'm going to help you, I need to ask questions and do some investigating. How else am I going to find a loophole? And, to be honest, I think we may have found one. Where was Peter Hayden on the day of your parents' deaths?"

"So, what are you proposing? That he came over, found my mother like that in the tub, then killed my father?"

"Could be."

"But there was no forced entry."

"So, maybe your dad let him in for some totally unrelated reason. Maybe Hayden then revealed who he was and killed your father in the heat of the moment? What if your mother didn't know how to deal with your father's death, took some pills, and then got into the tub? What if she even committed suicide to take the rap?"

Julian sits down beside me again and stares out into space. "So what now? Ask more questions? Go back to the ranch? I really don't think that's smart."

"You can't live in this barn forever, Julian. What happens when my dad comes back for his power tools? Or my mom goes looking for her gardening gloves?"

"I really want to trust you."

I reach out to touch his wrist, running my fingers over the pickax tattoo. "So, trust me to dig up the truth."

He looks at me. There's a startled expression in his eyes. "Just promise me."

"What?"

His mouth trembles open, but he doesn't utter another sound. He looks so fragile—like he could collapse from a single nudge.

I rest my head against his shoulder, able to see the motion in his chest. "I promise," I say, not finishing my thought either. But maybe the silent vow is enough for the moment.

We don't speak again until it's time for me to go—until I hear the slam of Mom's car door in the driveway.

"Good night," I say, hating to pull away.

"Good night." He musters a smile. His voice is soft, like velvet.

If only I could curl up inside his voice.

If only there could be another way.

thirty-eight

Later, in my room, I empty my bag. It's full of Peter Hayden's receipts. I collect them in a heap on my bed, cringing at the thought of having left some behind—on the floor, under his desk, behind the door.

How long would it take for him to find a couple? To notice the folder's missing? And then to ask the woman at the desk if anyone went into his office? How long after that would a lightbulb click above the woman's head, remembering my visit?

Remembering me.

I sift through the pile, trying to put the receipts in order, from January until the present. The whole reason I took the folder was to see if there might've been any romantic purchases made—flowers, candy, dinners, trips—hoping to prove somehow that Hayden was still seeing Julian's mother.

Most of the receipts are for obvious work-related expenses: hay, feed, grooming supplies, cleaning stuff. I form a series of stacks. There have got to be at least three hundred pieces of paper here, small ones, full sheets, in every color of the rainbow.

Finally, after about forty minutes of searching, I find it: the needle in the haystack. Not a romantic purchase, but one made on Saturday, May 4.

The heading on the receipt says Wallington Hardware. The purchase was made in the morning, at nine a.m., and paid for in cash. There are two five-digit strings of numbers, for each of the items bought. The prices are $17.99 and $29.99.

I grab my laptop and search for Wallington Hardware's contact information. It closed two hours ago. I type one of the item numbers into the product search box. An error message pops up right away, informing me that the item cannot be located. I try the other number. The same message appears.

I attempt to do a Google search, but nothing relevant comes up—just real estate stuff (address numbers and area codes).

It'll have to wait until tomorrow.

Wednesday, October 21

Night

I stood outside the bathroom and knocked on the door. There was a puddle at my feet. Water had seeped beneath the door, sopping into the rug.

"Mom?" I shouted, jiggling the knob. When she didn't answer, I shoved my weight against the door panel until it finally gave way.

Mom was lying in a tub of water. Her body had sunk beneath the surface.

I saw her eyes first: piercing green, angled up toward the ceiling. I told myself it wasn't her. I mean, it couldn't possibly be her. This couldn't possibly be real.

She was still in her nightgown from that morning. Her slippers were still on her feet. Water spilled over the porcelain rim. Splash. Splash. At least three inches on the floor. A couple of empty pill bottles floated too. Painkillers, antidepressants.

I can't describe what I felt in that moment. It was like every horrible experience I'd ever had hitting me at the same time—only it was worse than that.

I sank to the floor, able to hear my father's voice playing in my ear: "Steven would've been a far better son than you."

I'm not sure how long I stayed like that—if it was for an hour or a minute—before I shut the water off. The silence made things worse somehow.

I tried to pull her out. Her limbs were already stiff. Water gushed over the rim, over me. I held her body in my arms. She was so tiny. Her ribs poked through the fabric of her nightgown. The bones in her neck were almost visible through the skin. Why hadn't I done more to help her?

Why hadn't she done more to help me?

thirty-nine

It's early morning, before school, and Mom's in the kitchen making breakfast.

"Waffles on a weekday? What's the special occasion?" I ask her.

"I couldn't sleep. I have a meeting with a new client, and then I have to work late again tonight." She's dressed in her navy blue pantsuit (the one she reserves for all-important meetings), and her hair's hiked up in a bun. "Syrup? Nutella? Whipped cream?" She's standing over the plate of waffles, armed with all three.

Before I can answer, the doorbell rings. My insides jump.

Mom's eyebrow darts up in suspicion. "I'll take that as a 'none of the above' on the waffle toppings. You're jittery enough without the added sugar. Better to just eat them straight up. Now, would you mind getting the door?"

I head for the front entrance, wondering who it could possibly be at this hour. Standing on tiptoes, I look through the peephole.

Max is there.

Still dressed in my sweats from bed, I open the door. "Hey," I say, stepping aside to invite him in. "You're up early."

"I have an early-morning soccer practice." He hands me a cup of coffee. "Let's try this again, shall we? Me bringing you coffee, that is, without any weirdness."

"I take full blame for the weirdness. I think I must've been temporarily body-snatched by the aliens of Planet Bizarro."

"There's a response to a kiss that I haven't heard before. Most girls just don't answer my calls."

"Max—" I cringe. "That's not what I meant."

"I know." He smiles. "Anyway, I'm sorry that I was such an ass when you came to talk to me before class."

"It's fine. I deserved the asshole treatment. Oh, wait"—my face goes fireball red—"that totally didn't sound right."

Max laughs. "But I didn't come here just to apologize and bring you coffee."

"You didn't?" I bristle slightly, afraid he might still be getting the wrong message.

"I was hoping you wouldn't mind if I still went to that party with Jeannie. I mean, if it's weird, please say so. It's just—"

"It's not weird at all," I say, cutting him off.

"Okay, cool." He smiles. "And, of course, you're welcome to come too. It's just that she asked me. Last night. On the phone. And, I don't know, but I was pretty excited she wanted to go."

"*So* cool," I agree, psyched to hear that Jeannie called him. "You guys will have a great time together."

Max smiles wider, seemingly relieved. I'm relieved as well, and not just because he's no longer upset, but because maybe—finally—we've arrived at a mutual place.

After he leaves, and once Mom's gone off to work, I head out to the barn, en route to school, with a plate full of waffles. I rap lightly. Julian opens the door. The sight of him, despite my unending questions, makes my entire body quake.

"Good morning," he says.

I force myself to look away. "Breakfast?"

He takes the plate. But still I linger in the doorway, half wanting to go in, but knowing I should go.

"Did you want to come in for something?" he asks.

I open my mouth to tell him no, but instead I step inside. His journal is open on the floor. I rack my brain for something to ask him—some detail about the case, some reason beyond waffles for me to even be here right now. "Will I ever get to read your writing?"

He sets the waffles down and comes a little closer.

"Do you ever write about us?" I ask, before he can answer. "About our time together, I mean?"

Julian takes my hand and traces the lines of my palm. "What do *you* think?"

I swallow hard, looking down at our hands, knowing I'm in way over my head.

"So, I was just kind of wondering..."

"What?" I ask.

"Who's that guy?"

"That guy?"

He peeks up from my palm. "The one who drives the Jeep."

"Oh." My heart hammers. "He's just a friend."

The tiniest of grins forms across his lips. "So I guess I'll see you later. After school."

But I don't want to go. I squeeze his hand, and he draws me slightly toward him. His mouth is so close—just a hairbreadth from mine—that if either of us were to speak another word, our lips would bump together.

I close my eyes, feeling the warmth of his breath smoke against my mouth.

"You should go," he says, taking a step back, and making my heart squelch.

Still, I know.

It's true.

He's absolutely right.

I turn away and slip out the door, grateful to him for halting the moment, disappointed in myself for not.

forty

All during school, I try my best to concentrate on the case. In my study block, I go over my audio transcripts, come up with a list of more questions, reread news reports, and create a timeline for Saturday, May 4.

But then my mind wanders back to this morning—what coud've happened, that almost-kiss.

And all other thinking stops.

After school, in my room, I grab Hayden's file folder and open it up. The receipt from Wallington Hardware is sitting on top. I dial the store's number. A male voice answers right away.

"Hi. I'm wondering if you could help me," I begin. "I have

a receipt for a couple of purchases I made at your store back in May. I'm trying to figure out what they were. It's sort of a long story." I fake a laugh. "But I have the item numbers and I was hoping that you could look them up."

"Wait, are you looking to make a return? Just bring in the unopened items, along with the receipt."

"No. I'm not making a return. I want to figure out what I bought. I have the item numbers," I tell him again.

"Um, okay. But I'm not really sure how to do that."

"I think you can just type the numbers in. I've seen people do that."

"Wait, can you hold on for a second?"

"Sure." I sigh, hoping that someone's there to help him.

He comes back on the line a few moments later. "The manager will be in tomorrow. Do you think you could call back then? Sorry, I'm new here."

"Okay," I say, thoroughly disappointed.

I hang up and head down to the kitchen to fix dinner for Julian, reminding myself that I need to stay focused on the case. I can't be getting emotionally involved. I cross the yard to the barn, wondering if I should broach the "need-to-stay-focused" topic, but the door opens before I can decide.

Julian looks just as amazing as he did this morning, with his wide brown eyes and perfectly rumpled hair. There's a thin layer of stubble over his chin and cheeks.

"Could we talk some more?" I ask, handing him a bag of food and closing the door behind me.

We sit down across from each other, and I do my best to avoid looking into his face, or staring at his mouth. Instead, I take out the tape player, putting a palpable wedge between us, and push RECORD.

ME: I need you to remember back. Is there anything at all— ticket stubs, restaurant receipts, lies your mother told— that might've suggested that she and Peter Hayden were still dating these past couple of years?

JULIAN: My mom hadn't been well these past couple of years. She barely even left the house.

ME: But you were in school most of the day. Is there a chance someone might've visited her while your dad was at work?

JULIAN: I suppose there's a chance, but I really don't think she was still seeing that guy.

ME: Because . . .

JULIAN: She was frail. She barely spoke. She slept most of the time.

ME: All because of your father?

JULIAN: He certainly didn't help.

ME: Can we talk about the way your father treated you? You said before that he would often compare you to Steven—the person he imagined that Steven would become.

JULIAN: That's right.

ME: Why do you think he did that?

JULIAN: Hell if I know. Maybe to put distance between us. Maybe if he didn't love me, it wouldn't have been hard to lose me if something happened.

ME: What were you and your father fighting about on the day of his death?

JULIAN: It was just something that he said.

ME: What did he say?

JULIAN: . . .

ME: Julian?

JULIAN: He said he wished that it was Steven who lived and . . .

ME: What?

JULIAN: And me who died.

ME: He probably wasn't thinking when he said it.

JULIAN: He knew what he was saying. He said it all the time, blaming me for taking Steven's car seat and distracting Mom from driving that day. He said it was because of me that she hit the tree.

ME: You know those things aren't true though, right?

JULIAN: . . .

ME: Julian?

JULIAN: Steven should've been the one to live.

I press PAUSE. Julian's turned away now.

"I know this must be hard," I say, referring to his openness. I'm not his journal; he's probably never told these things to anyone. "But you have to understand: your father comparing you to Steven... it wasn't rational. He was making comparisons about things that hadn't even happened yet, not giving you a chance to grow into the person you were meant to be."

Julian shrugs. "My dad comparing me to Steven, it just became normal."

"Do you see now that it's not?" I reach out to touch his hand, stopping him from picking at the skin on his palm.

He turns to look at me. His eyes are red. He's holding back tears. "What is it like to be normal—the way normal is for you?"

"Who's to say that *my* normal is the *right* normal?"

"It's got to be a whole lot 'righter' than mine."

"So, let's be normal," I say, without a second thought.

His face furrows. He doesn't get what I mean. I'm not sure I get it either. Still, I go for the bag of clothes, pulling out the pair of jeans from yesterday and the blue waffle top. "Put these on," I tell him. "I have some other things in my room."

"What for?"

"Just do it." I head back to the house before he can argue.

forty-one

"Are we done yet?" Julian asks, sitting on a toolbox in lieu of a makeup chair.

I apply a thick layer of concealer to mask the scar beneath his eye. I follow up with foundation across his cheeks, to hide the spray of freckles.

"Now?" he asks.

"Almost," I say, pulling a knitted hat over his head to completely cover his hair. I also give him a pair of clunky black nonprescription eyeglasses, fished from our Halloween costume bin, and a puffy winter jacket to add layers to his midsection.

"Can I look?"

I hold the hand mirror up to show him.

"Wow," he says, pushing the glasses up farther on his face. "But I still don't know if this is a good idea."

"It'll only be for a couple of hours. Come on," I say, taking his hand and leading him outside.

We leave the barn just as it's turning dark, and walk along the bike path toward town. Julian barely says two words the entire way there. He just keeps looking up at the sky, waiting for the sun to go down altogether.

"Don't worry," I try to assure him. "No one's going to recognize you."

I pick a pizza place on the fringe of town, behind the local college campus. It's always full of college students, so I never know anyone here. We slip inside, and I make a beeline for a two-seater table in the far back corner. I take the seat that faces outward, while Julian sits with his back to the other tables.

The waitress comes right away, not even giving Julian a second glance. She hands us the menus and then scurries on her way.

"Good?" I ask him.

"Weird." He smiles.

"Normal," I say, correcting him.

We order a caramelized-onion pizza with a side of curly fries and two limeades. And we start off by talking about *normal* stuff—like favorite foods and best ice cream. Him: enchiladas and fudge ripple. Me: veggie pad thai and butter pecan.

"So, what's the one thing you're most excited to do or see once all of this legal stuff gets cleared?" I ask him.

"*If* it gets cleared, you mean."

"Finish school? Go on a vacation? Walk down the street without having to wear three inches of makeup and clunky glasses?"

"I don't know." He toys with the prongs of his fork. "I guess I don't really have any expectations."

"In other words, there's nothing you'd do if you could?"

"I'd love to go to the beach again. Pretty basic, I know, but it's sort of my special place, where I've always felt most safe. When I was little, I used to want to be a lifeguard."

"So that you could save other people?"

"Maybe." He shrugs. "I guess. I never stopped to think about it."

"And what do you want to do now?"

"I don't really dwell on what I want to do for work. I mostly just think about the kind of person I want to be."

"And what kind of person is that?"

"More like you, actually." He sets his fork down.

"Seriously?" I ask, waiting for the punch line.

"Absolutely serious." He stares at me from behind the black

rims; they make the gold in his eyes look brighter. "It's pretty amazing the way you help people, without looking for something in return. I hope that doesn't weird you out."

"It's actually pretty flattering. I mean, I've never really thought of myself as anything other than ordinary."

"Well, you should," he says, gazing at my mouth. "Because you're the most incredible person I've ever met."

My insides warm up like toast, and I don't know how to respond. While he's been wanting to feel normal, I've been striving to be *super*-normal—as if normal isn't good enough. As if *I* have never been good enough.

Our food and drinks arrive. The waitress pushes aside the floral arrangement on our table to make room for the plates.

"Forget-me-nots," I say, catching Julian admiring the tiny blue petals.

"I guess someone knows her flowers."

"Only because I used to photograph them."

"A perfect choice for our table, don't you think?" He smiles.

I smile too. Things are just as I'd hoped. The food is good. Julian is relaxed. There's not a single soul I recognize or who recognizes us.

But then the door jingles open.

And Tori walks in.

She's with that Bojo guy from the Ragdoll. They search around for a table. Meanwhile, my body instantly shrinks. I look downward, sipping my drink, paranoid she might recognize him from the convenience store and put two and two together.

"What's wrong?" Julian asks.

I peek back up. Tori's looking in my direction. She waves. I wave back. And then she crosses the restaurant toward me.

I straighten back up, unable to help noticing that she's dressed like Frida Kahlo, with a big red scarf, a blue floral dress, and flowers in her hair.

"Fancy finding you here," she says, standing at our table. But she's not even looking at me; she's completely focused on Julian. "Aren't we one for secrets."

"Hey," Julian says to her. "I'm James."

"Tori," she says, extending her hand for a shake. "Have we met? Because you look so familiar. Debate team? Middle school?"

"I don't think so." Julian bows his head slightly.

Finally, she looks back at me. "I think we definitely have some catching up to do."

"Well, you've been pretty preoccupied."

"Right," she says, taking Bojo by the hand. He's wearing striped harem pants and a matching hat that looks like a tissue box. "We're just grabbing a quick bite before our movie."

"Well, we were just finishing up." Julian nods to the half-eaten pizza.

"You *do* look really familiar," Bojo tells him. "Do you go to Crest Hill?"

Julian shakes his head.

"Well, I never forget a face, especially not this one," he says, turning to Tori. He smells the flowers in her hair and then kisses her cheek—not once but *three* times. "Table?"

"Definitely," she purrs.

While they head off to a booth, Julian and I pack up and leave. It's completely dark out now, making the air seem suddenly cooler.

We walk along the sidewalk, toward the south end of the street, and once again Julian has fallen silent.

"Did Tori and her friend bother you?" I ask him. "The stuff they said about never forgetting a face?"

"How could it not? I mean, I'm really out on a limb here."

"By being outside, you mean?"

"By all of it: being outside, befriending you, talking about stuff that no one else really knows."

I stop him from walking by grabbing his forearm. The clock on the bell tower chimes, reminding me that we don't have time to waste. "But all of that stuff—opening up, being vulnerable, trusting others, forming relationships—that's normal too."

Julian stares at me—*hard*—studying my every blink and breath. "I have to go back, you know. You have your own life. And I can't pretend to be anyone other than—"

"I've never asked you to pretend. And you don't have to go back right now."

"You're right." He takes my hand and brings me across the street.

We continue for four more blocks, before he leads us between two houses, where there's a pathway made of beach shells. We move down a grassy hill, and the ocean makes its appearance. The moon shines over it, painting stripes on the incoming waves. I take a few pictures, including one of Julian, able to smell the sea-tangled air.

"Zigmont Beach," he says. "Ever come here?"

I shake my head.

"So then what are we waiting for?"

I hop onto the sandy beach and kick off my shoes. There isn't a single other soul here. I gaze back at the row of houses behind us. A couple of them have their porch lights on. Some one's barbecuing food. There's music playing in the distance—a flute, a piano, a violin. People are enjoying life.

People, including us.

Julian takes off the hat and glasses and begins toward the water. The cool beach sand feels like powder beneath my feet. We roll up our jeans and sit by the ocean's edge.

"Thanks for letting me bring you here," he says. "The ocean always makes me feel invincible somehow—like anything is possible."

"Anything *is* possible."

"You make me feel that way too."

My heart pounds in response. "I know something that'll make you feel even more invincible. Ever hear of the polar bear plunge?"

He shakes his head.

"Okay, well, technically, it's a *pre*–polar bear plunge, since it's not winter yet, and normally there's a fund-raising component, but we can just skip that part."

"Okay," he says, but still there's a question on his face.

"So, let's take the plunge." I get up and nod toward the water.

"You can't be serious."

"You're not chicken, are you?"

"Hell, no," he says, getting up too. He peels off the waffle shirt, revealing a thin white tee.

I follow suit, pulling off my sweater, leaving the tank top underneath.

Julian kicks off his boots and wriggles out of his jeans. I take my jeans off too, trying not to peek at his boxers, unable to help staring at his legs—the muscles in his calves, the hair sprouting from his skin—all the while tugging at the length of my tank.

"Last one in is a polar bear," I shout, running for the water.

Julian follows. We splash through the incoming waves.

Together, we swim out, toward the moon. The water is absolutely freezing, but there's warmth here too.

"So, now what?" Julian asks.

"That's it. We took the plunge."

"So now we leave?"

"Yeah." I shrug, twitching from the cold.

He moves a little closer—until we're standing just a few inches apart. "Except I don't want to leave just yet." He reaches out, finding my hands beneath the water.

I weave my fingers through his, wishing he could be someone else—even for a moment—rather than this person on the run, this person I'm trying to help.

The moon lights up the sharp angles of his face. "We're from two entirely different worlds," he says.

But that doesn't change how I feel.

Julian clenches his teeth and looks away. Perhaps he's just as conflicted. Still, all I can think about is wrapping my arms around him. And never letting go.

I feel myself floating toward him, forcing him to look at me.

"Day," he whispers into my ear. His breath is against my neck. "We should stop."

"I know."

He takes a step back. His eyes meet mine. But I draw him closer again and press my lips against his cheek, able to feel his heart throbbing against my chest.

His hands encircle my waist. My leg tangles with his as I swallow him up in my arms, melting into his embrace.

"Just this once," I whisper.

He nods slightly. His lips graze mine—once, twice, three full times—before he kisses me, finally. And it tastes like warm, salted caramel inside my mouth, over my tongue, awakening an aching deep inside me.

His hands cradle my face. His fingers glide down my spine, beneath my tank, all over my skin. If I didn't know better, I'd think the heat between the two of us could set this ocean on fire.

He lifts me upward and I wrap my legs around his waist, wishing I could take the picture, desperate to capture the moment. As if moments could ever be captured. As if time could somehow stand still.

Thursday, October 22

Afternoon

I was nine years old the first time I saw my mother's scars. On her wrists. Thick red slash marks, crusted over with dried blood.

She was crouched beneath the picnic table, still dressed in her nightgown from the morning, even though it was approaching nighttime.

"What happened?" I asked, joining her under the table, nodding to the cuts.

"Just a scrape." Her eyes were vacant—so far gone from all her pills.

There was a hole in the soil between us. Inside was a beaded bracelet that Dad had given her for a wedding present, as well as a couple of her pills, and one of Steven's baby socks. Tiny scraps of paper lined the walls of the hole. Scribbled across them were the words GUILT, MARRIAGE, FEAR, *and* MY LIFE.

"Can I have a slip of paper?" I asked her.

"Sure." She brightened. There were dried up tear tracks down her cheeks. "What would you like to bury?"

"Dad," I told her.

She didn't so much as flinch, just handed me the pen. I wrote his name down. She kissed my cheek. Then, together, we refilled the hole.

forty-two

After school the following day, I check my phone, noticing a missed call. I don't recognize the number, but still I press it to dial, wondering if it might be Barry's.

"Hello?" A male voice.

"Hi, I think you called me?"

The phone goes radio silent.

"Hello?" I ask.

"Yeah," he says. "I heard you're doing an assignment on Julian Roman's case."

"That's right. Is this Barry?"

"Which college?"

"Crest Hill State University. Would it be okay if I asked you some questions?"

"Not over the phone. Let's meet someplace. I've got some free time now."

"Um, sure," I say, completely *un*sure. My tape recorder's back at home. But still I don't want to miss this opportunity. "Where?"

"Orange Park? I'll be on one of the benches by the dog park."

I agree and hang up, both anxious and excited to question him. I cross the street in front of the school and take the number-four bus into the town of Decker. On the way, I do a search of the local headlines with Julian's name, looking for any updates.

An article pops up right away. It was posted just this morning:

SEARCH CONTINUES FOR TEEN
ACCUSED OF HOMICIDE

WEBER, MA—The search continues for Julian Roman, 16, of Decker Village Park. Roman was reported missing from the Fairmount County Juvenile Detention Facility on October 6, while awaiting trial for the alleged murder of his father. Officials know Roman escaped from the courtyard through a section of wire fencing compromised during construction. Roman is reported to have dark hair and eyes, an athletic build, and to be six feet tall. He was last seen on surveillance video taken from a convenience store in Bethel, wearing gray pants and a hooded sweatshirt. Officials have reason to believe he's still in the Bethel area, and urge anyone who might have information about his whereabouts to contact their local police department.

I click off my phone, feeling my stomach twist. Officials have reason to believe he's still in the Bethel area? What is their reason? Didn't the police say that someone fitting Julian's description was spotted in the town of Millis?

About forty minutes later, the bus pulls over in front of the park's entrance gates. I get out. The doors close behind me with a hard, heavy thwack. The park looks smaller than I remember it last—fewer benches, not as many trees. There's a skating rink in the center that my parents used to take me to when I was first learning to Rollerblade. It looks smaller too.

I peer all around, spotting the dog park in the corner. I move in that direction, scanning all of the benches. I'm just about to walk around the perimeter of the gate.

But then: "Day?"

I whirl around. The boy from the coffee shop is sitting on the ground, beneath a tree. I recognize him right away: the faux-hawk hair, his olive skin. Dressed in baggy jeans and a zip-up sweatshirt, he comes and extends his hand toward me.

"Barry?" I shake his hand.

"Yeah. You're a lot different than I pictured."

"What did you picture?"

"I don't know. Some mousy college girl, I guess." He laughs. "By the way, I think it's way cool that you're researching Julian's case for an assignment. For once, schoolwork that actually has a point."

I take a notebook and pen from my bag.

"Julian is a really good friend of mine," Barry continues. "We grew up together, in the same neighborhood."

"So you know his parents?"

"I know everything," he says, giving me a pointed look.

"Well, then can you please explain why he was arrested in the first place? Because I'm having a hard time trying to piece together enough of a reason. So much seems circumstantial."

"Do you mind if we walk and talk?" He gazes over his shoulder at the street. "I think better when I'm in motion."

"Sure," I say, following him toward the exit gate.

There are cars whizzing by on the main road, and a strip of shops in the distance. The smell of car exhaust is thick in the air. Barry stuffs his hands into the pockets of his jacket, and we walk along the sidewalk, toward a major intersection.

"First, I just want to say that I don't think Julian's guilty. I mean, yes, he hated his dad pretty hard-core, but who didn't? The guy was a total asshole. But did Julian kill the dude? That just doesn't seem like something that Julian would do."

"And so who do *you* think killed Mr. Roman?"

"Julian's a good guy," he says, in lieu of a response. "But he got a really raw deal—not just with this case. His life has always been pretty shitty. A real shame, too—the guy is, like, a genius. Not many people know that."

"He'd have to be smart to escape a detention facility and remain on the run."

We come to the end of the sidewalk, and Barry crosses the main road.

"Where are we going?" I ask him.

"Just a little bit farther," he says, turning down Cherry Street. It's a relatively quiet road, with cars lining both sides and a gas station on the far corner.

"*Where?*" I insist.

He doesn't answer, just keeps on moving, his pace quickening with every step. I'm almost tempted to turn around, but I stay beside him for a few more blocks, my cell phone clenched in my hand.

I look upward. The clouds have collected over us, and it suddenly appears darker. "*Barry?*" I demand.

He stops, finally, and turns to me. "This is it," he says, nodding to the house.

We're standing directly in front of it.

I recognize the house from news articles: the yellow police tape, the screened-in front porch, the faded white shingles. "Julian's house," I mutter.

"I thought that coming here might give you a better picture of things."

"It does," I say, trying to imagine Julian coming home from the beach that day, parking his car out front, and climbing up the broken steps.

"I live just around the corner."

"And the neighbor whose lawn Julian mowed?"

Barry points to a red Victorian across the street and a few houses down. "The guy's pretty nice, but he's hardly ever home."

"If he's hardly ever home, how can he say for sure what time Julian mowed his lawn?" Not that it even matters much.

"Apparently the wife came home for lunch around noon and the grass wasn't cut."

"But that's still hearsay if nobody else can corroborate the detail."

"You sound like a cop."

"I actually sound a lot like my mother."

"Is *she* a cop?"

"No. She's just good at picking stories apart, catching people in lies."

"That must suck for you." He laughs.

I gaze back at the house. The windows look vacant—no curtains, nothing propped on the sill. The mailbox hangs crooked by the door, its flag pointed downward. "I wish I could see inside."

Barry glances over both shoulders before pulling a knife from his back pocket. "Come on," he says, moving to the side of the house.

I remain firmly in place, watching as he walks along a row of bushes that separates the Romans' land from the neighbor's.

"We'll just have ourselves a little peek," he says, stopping in front of the window toward the back. He cuts a couple of the police tape ribbons.

I grab the keys in my pocket and run my finger over the sharpest one, ready to use it if I need to. I begin toward him, my curiosity piqued.

Barry points inside. "This is Julian's bedroom."

I peer through the glass, keeping Barry in my peripheral vision, especially since he's still holding the knife. Four stark white walls surround two single beds, a broken dresser with lopsided drawers, and a trash barrel that only partially covers a gaping hole in the carpet.

"See... nothing out of the ordinary," Barry says.

"I guess." If ordinary is a room that resembles a prison cell.

"The bed on the right was Steven's." He points to it. There's a stack of storybooks where there should be a pillow. "Do you know about Julian's brother that died?"

I nod. "Someone in the group found out about him somewhere."

"Yeah, sucks. When Steven died, it pretty much killed the family."

"Did you know Julian back then?"

"Yeah. We weren't in school yet, but we played together—with Steven too. I remember that Steven had the funniest laugh, more like a cackle, and always carried fake bugs in his pockets."

"Do you remember a change in the parents after Steven's death?"

"I remember that Mrs. Roman went pretty quiet and stopped inviting me over for lunch, and that Mr. Roman would flip out over the littlest thing—like this one time when I sat down on Steven's bed. The guy went totally ballistic."

"Do you think Mrs. Roman could've killed her husband?"

"You obviously never met Mrs. Roman." He laughs. "People called her the walking zombie, because she was ninety pounds and completely checked out on painkillers. If you so much as sneezed in her direction, she would've fallen down."

"So maybe she threw something heavy at his head."

"Not with enough force that it would've killed him. Apparently forensics investigators were able to estimate the force that hit Mr. Roman—something to do with weight and speed. Anyway, they said that Mrs. Roman wasn't physically capable."

"How do you know all this?"

"Julian told me, before the arrest. He used to tell me everything." He taps the blade of his knife against his chin in thought. "My theory: she either offed herself once she saw her dead husband, or she did it earlier, before he was killed, which would explain Mr. Roman's really bad mood that day."

"Bad mood?"

"You didn't hear about the UPS guy witness?"

"Oh, right. Julian and his father's argument-turned-fight."

"I figure the fighting must've been pretty explosive. Why else would the UPS guy go spying in the windows?"

"Did the UPS guy call the police?"

"Nope. And I'll bet he's lost a few good nights' sleep over that, because imagine if he *had* called. The police would've appeared on the scene. No chance for a homicide with cops hanging around to mess it all up." He laughs again. "Did anyone in your group find out about the fingerprints?"

I shake my head.

"Yeah, I guess nobody really knows about that. The police didn't leak it."

"Leak *what*?"

Still holding the knife, Barry places his hands around his

neck in a choke hold, rolls his eyes upward, and sticks his tongue out to be funny. "There were fingerprints found around Mr. Roman's throat."

"Wait, *what*?"

"They were on some necklace he was wearing, as well as on his skin. I know, right? Who knew you could get prints off skin, but apparently it's possible. Something about sweat residue, lipids, and amino acid shit—way too science-class for my taste." He laughs some more. "Anyway, they were Julian's fingerprints—and not from a pulse-check, if you get what I'm saying."

The detail goes straight through my chest, like a sharp-pointed spike.

"I know, freakin' sucks, right?" he says.

"It had to have been some mistake. Maybe Julian had touched his father's neck earlier in the day."

"I take it your group is Team Julian, then?" He grins.

"I'm just trying to play devil's advocate."

"The prints were made from the front, with the thumbs right between the clavicle. But, even so, all the prints prove is that Julian was trying to defend himself from his father's bullshit."

"I thought his father was killed from a blunt trauma to the head?"

"He was."

I shake my head. "Then I guess I'm even more confused."

"The police think that Julian tried to strangle his father," he explains, using his knife-holding hand. "But then when that didn't work, he grabbed something in the heat of the moment and hit him over the head."

"And you know all of this because...?"

"Like I said, Julian told me everything. He said his father had him pinned that day, and so he had no choice but to try and protect himself. When I asked him—for the millionth time— if he killed his father, even by accident, he said he didn't. He swears he left the house after the fight. He says he went for a ride, looking for me, but I was at work at the restaurant. It wasn't until Julian got back home that he found the bodies."

"Wow," I say, taking his words in, feeling my pulse race.

"I know. But, hey, three cheers for no murder weapon yet, right? At least we've got that going for us."

"Do we even know what the murder weapon is?"

"No." He sighs. "And believe me, the police have looked." He moves to another window—the one that's closer to the street.

I follow along and look inside. The living room's been ransacked, the sofa cushions thrown askew. An end table drawer's been dumped out onto the floor.

Barry smooshes his face up against the glass, making a weird humming sound as he does.

"All these theories..." I turn toward him again, noticing

how he's frequently looking upward, avoiding eye contact. "What's your theory on who did it?"

"Hell if I know." He uses the back end of the knife to scratch his forehead. "But his dad wasn't exactly short on enemies, myself included."

"Okay, but being an enemy doesn't mean that you want to kill that person."

"You might've asked me that question about six months ago, when he shoved me up against a fence and said that I was a worthless piece of shit. Thankfully I have an alibi for his death; I was at work. Otherwise, who knows; maybe they'd have locked my ass up too."

"Someone in our group said that Mrs. Roman might've had a boyfriend."

"Yeah, but that was years ago, at least according to Julian. But who knows? Maybe that's just what she told him. But, then again, who would date a zombie?"

"Is it possible that a former lover might've sought retaliation for Mrs. Roman's zombie state?"

"*Bam,*" he says, using his knife as a baseball bat through the air. "I think you might be on to something. Is that what your group thinks?"

"We're exploring all possibilities, including the one that involves Mrs. Roman seeking help in the death of her husband."

"Help as in a hit man? I'd give that lady major props if that were true."

"Do you know if the police questioned the neighbors to see if anyone was spotted coming into or out of the house?"

"Yes, and negative. But then again, half the neighbors here are drunk by two in the afternoon. The other half don't want any dealings with the cops."

A police siren sounds in the distance. Barry scurries to bury his knife inside his boot. "We should go."

I start to mutter a good-bye, but Barry has already turned away and headed for the street.

forty-three

Instead of taking the bus to the stop by my house, I get out in the center of town and walk three blocks to my dad's new apartment. It's sandwiched between the movie theater and a French bakery, which, admittedly, gives it a definite edge.

I search the door buzzers for my dad's name. It's there, in bold black typeface. I press it and wait for him to appear.

"Hey!" His face brightens when he sees me. He pulls me in, gives me a hug. He smells like the cologne version of grapefruit. "I'm so glad you came. I wasn't sure." He checks his watch.

"I made a detour first."

"Well, I'm really glad to see you." He leads me up a stairwell. "No elevators here. No need for a gym, either."

We climb four flights. The door to his new place is already open. I follow him inside. If I thought our house was sparsely decorated, Dad's apartment gives new meaning to the word "scant." There are two metal folding chairs positioned in front of a fuzzy green ottoman.

"Wow," I say, for lack of descriptive words.

"I know. I obviously have some work to do. But I was hoping that you could help me. We could go furniture shopping together."

"To make things more permanent?"

"I really want you to be comfortable here," he says, avoiding the question. "Come on, I'll give you a tour." He crosses the room and points to the kitchen.

From this angle, I can see a puke-green fridge and a tiled counter to match. The floor is the same as in the living room—wide-planked, dark-stained wood.

Dad points to two more rooms. "The one on the right is mine. Yours is on the left."

I move to have a look. The walls are painted lemon-yellow. There's also an armoire and a bed.

"It obviously needs decorating too," Dad says. "So start looking at catalogs to get ideas of what you might like."

"Why do *I* have a room here?" I ask, trying to process what all this means, as if it isn't already obvious. Dad's told me. I've clarified it. How many other ways do either of us have to say it?

My parents have grown apart. They're not getting back together—at least not anytime soon.

"You'll always have a place wherever I am," Dad says.

My eyes instantly fill, and I'm not even sure why. It's not just because of my parents' separation, or the fact that Dad has a new apartment, or that I have a room here.

It's everything. Just like Jeannie said. Life is changing, and I guess I'm having a hard time keeping up.

Dad comes and wraps his arms around me just as rain pelts down against the window screen behind him. "It's going to be okay. You'll see."

I wipe my eyes and take a step back. "I know. I just have a lot on my plate right now."

"With school? Your peace and justice club?"

I shake my head. "It's way more complicated than that."

"What is?"

Tears slide down my face. I take a seat on one of the metal folding chairs. "How do you do it?" I ask him. "How do you help people who've done bad things?"

He scoots down in front of me and takes my hand. "Where is all of this coming from?"

"I just don't get it." I shake my head. "You give those people a chance despite the fact that some of them have robbed banks or stolen cars. Or hurt others."

"I give them a chance because, in a lot of cases, they haven't been given one before."

"And what happens when they blow that chance—when you find out they're not the person that you thought?"

Dad gives my palm a squeeze. "Well, then that's a choice they've made today, and maybe tomorrow they'll choose more wisely. But at least I've given them some tools, as well as my trust and the benefit of the doubt. Believe it or not, those things are luxuries to some people—*gifts,* even. Has someone disappointed you?"

"Honestly, I don't know." All I know is that Julian's lied to me. Twice now. But does that make him guilty? Or does it just make things more complicated?

"Does whomever you're talking about need the kind of support I'm referring to?"

I bite the inside of my cheek, so tempted to spill my guts. "Do you think that good people can do bad things?"

"I know they can. Just look at your mother." He grins.

"Seriously now."

"I *am* being serious. Or maybe half-serious." Dad lets go of my hand and moves to sit on the fuzzy green ottoman, only it doesn't have enough stuffing, and he nearly topples off. "During some of her demonstrations, let's just say that things could get a little bit ugly. But *you've* heard the stories of throwing paint on strangers, linking arms across a highway, and destroying public property. Of course, for every one of those cases, she felt that her actions were justified. That's another tricky piece to all this. Everyone has their story—their own version of the truth, a rationale for how they act."

"Because everyone has a unique perspective," I say, thinking about my photo project.

"Exactly. In most cases, your mother's political escapades aside, I'd say that people act out when they've lost their way, or when they aren't getting the support they need. They've fallen through the cracks and gotten desperate. I'm not saying that what they do is justified, but you have to wonder: if those same people were given different opportunities—"

"They wouldn't rob banks?"

"Maybe or maybe not. The answers aren't so black and white, especially when there are other variables too, like mental illness, addiction, or trauma."

"Your clients are really lucky to have you."

"I'm lucky to have them too." He reaches out to take my hand again. "But I'm even luckier to have such an amazingly intelligent daughter, who asks all the right questions in her quest to do what's right." He holds my gaze for several seconds, perhaps waiting to see if I'll tell him what's *really* on my mind.

I clasp my hand around his, wondering if he'll persist with questions. But he doesn't—because maybe he trusts me to do the right thing, and that trust, as he said, feels like a gift unto itself.

There was a knock at the door, scaring me shitless, startling me awake. I sat up, all out of breath, and looked toward the window. It was dark out. The moon shone in through the glass, painting a narrow strip across the floor.

In the strip of light was a bag of supplies. A towel hung out. There were food cans on the floor and a pile of clothes. I was getting way too comfortable. I should've been ready to bolt at all times.

I got up and crept over to the window, tripping over a sand-bag, barely catching myself from falling forward. It was raining out. I angled my face against the glass, trying to see the door. But it was too dark.

Another knock.

"Julian?" Day's voice.

I went to the door and opened it an inch—just enough to assess the situation. It appeared that she was alone. She was standing there with a flashlight—not an umbrella—clenched in her hand. I widened the door to let her in, but she didn't move. Her face was wet from the rain. It looked like she'd been crying.

"Is there something you have to tell me?" she asked, before I could say hello.

Panic struck my heart like a match, burning through my veins, making my skin feel hot.

"Why didn't you tell me about the fingerprints around your father's throat, on his necklace?"

I clenched my teeth, wishing the floor would swallow me whole. More rain pelted down against her head, soaking her hair, draining down her neck.

"Just tell me. Is it true?"

My eyes slammed shut. Every inch of me shattered.

"They were your fingerprints?" she continued. "How could you leave a detail like that out? I trusted you to be honest with me." Her voice cracked over the words.

My heart cracked because I'd hurt her.

"So, now what?" she asked.

"It may sound selfish, but I didn't want you to know that about me."

Day shook her head and went back to the house, leaving me in darkness, taking all the light with her.

forty-four

I spend the following morning catching up on the non-Julian-related aspects of my life. I work on my photography project, finish my French and Chaucer essays, study for a physics exam, and call Jeannie to wish her luck on her date with Max tonight (at the "It's-Saturday-Let's-Party" party).

After lunch, in my room, I gaze out the window, feeling a gnawing sensation inside my gut. I haven't spoken to Julian since last night. But still I've been thinking about him.

A lot.

Am I surprised that he didn't tell me about the fingerprints? Someone who barely confided in anyone? Who writes his

feelings down in a notebook because that's safer than revealing them to other people?

No.

Not at all.

He hasn't been honest with me, but I'm not willing to give up
on his case. I'm way too invested now. Plus, it's no longer just
about him. This case is about me too—about having a sense of
purpose, and feeling as though what I'm doing matters.

I grab my camera and bag, then ask Mom to borrow her car
for a trip into town, which isn't entirely a lie. I will drive into
town, straight down Main Street, on my way to Wallington.

Mom says yes. I grab her keys. Wallington Hardware is a
tiny shop in the center of the city, about thirty minutes away.
I park right in front and fish Hayden's receipt from inside my
pocket. The doorbells chime as I enter the store. There's a
bearded guy at the counter.

"Can I help you?" he asks.

"I'm looking for the manager," I tell him.

An older woman emerges from the back room. She can't be
more than four feet nine, with hair hiked up in a cone-shaped
bun (perhaps to add a few more inches). "Look no further,"
she says.

"I bought a couple of items here back in May," I explain,
showing her the receipt. "I was hoping that you could tell me
what they were."

She gives me a befuddled look, with a creased forehead and pouty lips. Still, she goes behind the counter and types one of the item numbers into the register.

The register beeps. Words flash across the screen: PIPE, STEEL, 24-IN.

A shiver runs down my spine.

The woman raises an eyebrow at me. "Looks like you may have had some sort of plumbing issue back in May."

"Right." I nod. "Could you also check the other number? I don't remember what I bought with the pipe."

She types that number in too. "Gloves," she says, reading the screen.

"Gloves?"

"That's right." Her face furrows as she studies my expression. "Working gloves. Lots of people use them, including you if this is indeed your receipt."

Working gloves.

A steel pipe.

My head spins.

I feel my face flash hot.

"Anything else?" she asks.

"Could you tell me how heavy a twenty-four-inch steel pipe might be?"

She moves from around the counter and disappears down

one of the aisles, returning a few seconds later, holding a steel pipe. It's about three-fourths the length of a baseball bat. "Feel for yourself," she says, handing it to me.

I wrap my hand around it. It's easy to hold, about an inch and a half thick, and short enough to hide, but still it has ample weight, at least five pounds. Is it possible that Peter Hayden concealed a pipe like this behind his back, tucked inside his pants, with his shirt draped over the end? Was he wearing gloves at the time?

I pull my camera out of my bag and take several pictures of the pipe. "Would you mind showing me the gloves too?" I ask her.

The woman exchanges a look with the guy at the counter. "I must say, I've never had a customer take photos of items they purchased in the past. What is this *really* about?"

"A school project. Photography class."

Her eyes squint. I can tell she doesn't believe me. Still, she retrieves the gloves from one of the aisles: black leather, size large. I take a series of shots, suddenly noticing the surveillance camera over the cash register. Would the police watch the recording? Would the manager call them after I left?

"Thank you for your time." I snatch up the receipt and bolt for the door.

forty-five

Back in the car, I grab a notebook and add to my lists of facts and questions, trying my best to get a grip.

FACT: Peter Hayden bought a steel pipe and some construction gloves on the morning that his girlfriend's husband was killed.

FACT: Mr. Roman was hit over the head with a blunt object that's yet to be identified.

QUESTIONS: Could the purchases have been a coincidence? Does either of the above factors really mean that Peter Hayden is guilty?

I spend a few more moments coming up with a list of interview questions, then I grab my phone, as well as the tape recorder from my bag, and dial the number for Hayden's Ranch.

A woman answers.

"Could I please speak with Peter Hayden?" I ask her.

"Can I tell him who's calling?"

"Paula," I lie, pulling my tape recorder close.

The woman doesn't question it, just tells me to hang on. I push RECORD, set the phone to speaker mode, and take a deep and cleansing breath.

PETER HAYDEN (P.H.): Hello?

ME: Hi. Is this Peter Hayden?

P.H.: It is.

ME: A friend of mine took riding lessons with you a little while back and recommended that I do the same.

P.H.: What did you say your name was?

ME: Paula.

P.H.: And who was your friend?

ME: Her name was Jennifer Roman.

P.H.: . . .

ME: *Hello?*

P.H.: I don't give lessons, Paula.

ME: Did you use to—within this past year maybe? Because she said she took them from you.

P.H.: I haven't given lessons in a couple of years.

ME: *Really?* Because I didn't get the impression that it was *that* long ago.

P.H.: It's been a couple of years.

ME: Since you've seen Jennifer?

P.H.: . . .

ME: Do you think you could make an exception for the friend of a friend? I'd love to try a lesson, and she said I shouldn't go to anyone else.

P.H.: When did she say that?

ME: When I saw her last—maybe three or four months ago. It's taken me since then to muster up the nerve to go forward with this idea.

P.H.: Are you aware that Jennifer Roman passed away?

ME: Wait, *what*?

P.H.: She died, back in May.

ME: There must be some mistake.

P.H.: No mistake. I'm sure you can look it up online.

ME: I feel like I just saw her.

P.H.: Well, you haven't seen her since before May.

ME: How did she die?

P.H.: She took her own life.

ME: Oh my god.

P.H.: I'm sorry to have to be the one to tell you.

ME: I should've called her. I should've visited. I mean, I knew she was unhappy, but I never thought she'd . . .

P.H.: . . .

ME: When was the last time that *you* saw her?

P.H.: It'd been a while.

ME: More than five months, like me?

P.H.: . . .

ME: What was the date she died?

P.H.: Saturday, May fourth.

ME: Had you seen or talked to her that day?

P.H.: No.

ME: Because you were working? You work on Saturdays, right? That's what the woman at the front desk said.

P.H.: I wasn't working on *that* Saturday.

ME: Just by sheer coincidence?

P.H.: . . .

ME: *Hello?*

P.H.: Who is this?

ME: I told you already. My name is Paula.

P.H.: Who is this *really?*

ME: What were you doing on Saturday, May fourth?

P.H.: I've already spoken to the police.

ME: About an alibi? They questioned you?

P.H.: That's right. I was at home changing a gas pipe—not that it's any of your business.

ME: So you *don't* have an alibi for Saturday, May fourth. You were at home, all day?

P.H.: The police don't have anything on me, and neither do you, *Paula*. Now, I suggest that you hang up and forget we ever spoke.

ME: And if I don't?

P.H.: . . .

ME: *Hello?*

P.H.: Don't call back here again.

The phone clicks. I press STOP. My whole body chills.

I start the ignition and pull away from the curb, more suspicious than ever that he's getting away with murder.

forty-six

I come in through the front door, able to hear voices in the kitchen. Mom's talking to someone. There's a male voice—not my dad's. I head down the hallway to see who it is.

They're standing by the sink. Staring straight at me. The same two officers that were here before.

"What's going on?" I ask.

"We got a call," Officer Nolan says. She comes closer and flashes me a photo of Julian—the same one she showed me before.

"The boy from the convenience store." I nod. "His posters have been all over town."

"Do you know where he is?" the detective asks.

I shake my head, telling myself that I honestly can't be sure. He could be in the barn. He could also be in the woods. Or, maybe he ventured out on the bike path.

"We've already checked the barn." Detective Mueller gives me a knowing look, his eyebrows darted upward.

"Okay." I try my best to keep a poker face, but I can feel the emotion speckled across my neck, the bright red hives.

What did the officers see? Were they able to tell that Julian was here? Did Julian sweep up all the hair from when I cut it?

I peek over at Mom for help.

"You heard my daughter," she says. "She doesn't know where this boy is."

"Well, we still have more questions for her."

"Not now," Mom says, using the same assertive tone she reserves for her clients. "My daughter just got home, and I'd like to speak to her first."

"This will only take a few minutes," Mueller says.

"Well, then it can take a few minutes another time," Mom insists. "Need I remind you that she's a minor?"

Officer Nolan reaches for her card. "Please call us as soon as you can. The suspect is considered highly dangerous."

"As opposed to mildly dangerous?" Mom asks.

"This isn't a game," Nolan says. "If you *do* see him, call nine-one-one right away. Don't try to apprehend him on your own. I'll be following up before the end of the day."

Mom takes the card, and I move to the kitchen window to watch the officers leave. They cut across the yard, pausing in front of the barn before heading down the bike path.

Mom locks the door and turns to face me with her arms folded. "You have some explaining to do."

There's no point denying it: "I've been helping him."

"The boy they're looking for?"

I nod. "Julian Roman."

She clenches her teeth. "I don't even know what to say to you right now."

"Say that you love me and trust me, and that you know I'd never do anything I didn't believe was right."

She opens up a carton of eggs and breaks three of them into a pan, with the stove turned off, not even bothering to throw out the shells.

"At first I was just curious about his case," I venture. "He was a boy who seemed to need help. But then I got to know him..."

"And it became personal," she says, smashing another egg into the pan.

"I don't think he's gotten a fair deal."

"He hasn't been convicted yet, either. Why is he hiding instead of pleading his case, putting up a fight?"

"You know how it works without the right people in your corner. It's a losing battle."

"And where do *you* fit in?" she asks, picking the shells out of the pan.

"I've been gathering clues, offering support. He's been staying in the barn."

Mom turns to face me again. "So, now we're aiding and abetting?"

"You can just plead ignorance. It's more likely that I'd have kept Julian a secret."

"Which you did."

"Until now."

"I see." She sighs, folding her arms again. "Well, I don't think he'll be staying here much longer. The police will be back—with search warrants next time. And who knows about this phone call tip they got—who it's from and what they know."

"What did they find in the barn?"

"They didn't actually go inside. I caught them peeking through the windows. A sneaky pair too: they didn't even park out front; they must've hidden their car somewhere."

"So, where do we go from here?"

"You should've told me about him."

"I was respecting his privacy and giving him my trust—the way you do with your clients and the way Dad does with his."

Mom turns back to the pan of eggs, unable to deny it. "Well, I suspect your friend isn't stupid, since he's made it this long. He'll probably be on the run again—that is if he isn't already.

But if you really believe he's innocent, maybe there's something I can do to help." Her cell phone rings, cutting through our conversation. "Shit," she says, checking the screen. "I have to take this. It's about Pandora's case. But we're not finished yet, you hear me? I want to meet with this boy."

While she talks on the phone, I hurry out to the barn. I open the door and step inside.

Everything's been cleaned up, put back—like he was never even here. The clothes and blankets are collected in a corner. The food and water bottles are gone.

I grab the knitted blanket I lent him as tears roll down my face. There's a hollow sensation inside my heart. How could he leave? Just like that. Without even a hint of a good-bye.

forty-seven

It's one day later. Julian hasn't come back—at least not to stay. But this morning, when I passed by the barn on my way to take Gigi for a walk, there was a forget-me-not in the window box, making my heart instantly clench.

I peered over my shoulder before going to have a look. The whole window box had been filled with potting soil, the flower freshly planted. I moved closer to have a sniff. It smelled like honey. And reminded me of our date. I had to assume that Julian had done this—and that he was sending me a message.

He isn't far away.

The police have yet to follow up like they said they would.

Mom thinks it's because they don't have sufficient evidence to make a connection. "Of course, that also gives them all the more reason to find that evidence," she says.

It'll only be a matter of time.

Until then, while Mom's been busy with *her* case, I've been trying to find out more about mine. I picture myself going back to the horse ranch, talking to the woman at the desk again, and sneaking into Hayden's office. But what if my showing up there for a second time raises a red flag?

I resort to a Google search (to start with, anyway). In my room, I type a bunch of words into the search field:

Peter Hayden, Jennifer Roman

Peter Hayden, Michael Roman

Peter Hayden, homicide case

Peter Hayden, alibi

Peter Hayden, police questioning, alibi, May 4, Jennifer Roman

The latter combination of words does the trick. An article pops up about the case. It was published a few weeks after the crime. I'm pretty sure I've read this article before, from the *Decker Daily Journal*. But the part that I didn't read? A recent remark in the comments section. All of my words are highlighted:

I just heard that Peter Hayden was questioned about the Roman murder. Don't the police know what a lying son of a bitch he is? What's his alibi? Not that you could believe it. That crook has more friends in low places than I have credit card debt. I saw him and Jennifer Roman together a couple of summers ago. She didn't look well, but frankly I'd be sick too if I spent longer than two minutes in Hayden's company. No wonder she killed herself.

I close my laptop, not quite sure what to think. How is Peter Hayden supposedly a crook? And how did this person find out that Hayden was questioned by the police? My mind spinning with questions, I go into my virtual gallery, looking for a little diversion, not to mention a much needed brain break.

I have twelve pairs of photos for my project. I arrange them on the computer screen, starting with the snapshot of Jeannie— the one I took on our hike. She looks so peaceful, with the sun setting behind her, illuminating her skin. But in the next photo, as soon as she's turned her head, you can see the angst welled up in her eyes.

I've titled the project "My Excavation: An Exploration of Perspectives," because while some people dig to unearth the truth, others strive to bury it. I'm hoping to submit the project for consideration into the Shutter Exhibition at the Contemporary Art Institute. But before I do, there are just a couple more photos I need to get.

forty-eight

Instead of going home after school, I take the bus into the town of Decker and get out at the Orange Park stop—the same place that I met Barry.

I retrace my steps to Julian's house, feeling the rush of adrenaline the closer I get to his street. There's a police car parked in front of a drugstore on the main road. I readjust the scarf around my neck, trying to partially conceal my face, fearing it might be one of the officers that came to my house.

I duck down a narrow road that runs parallel to Julian's street, and then cut over, crossing two intersections, finally arriving by his house. The yellow police tape flaps in the wind, gets caught up in the bushes.

I grab my camera, feeling totally self-conscious. Standing at the corner of the property, I aim my lens at the front entrance, careful not to get the police tape, angling instead on the bright red door and the matching shutter beside it. An ivy plant snakes up the clapboard shingles. I retreat back a little, able to get that too, as well as a patch of wildflowers growing among the weeds.

I take a handful of more shots before pausing to check them out. The photos are just what I intended. They give the illusion of home.

My next series of photos uses a wider angle; it's the same view of the house, but also with the police tape; the overgrown lawn; and the wide, gaping hole in the porch lattice, like someone kicked it in.

I move around to the side of the house and aim my camera lens into the living room window, focusing on the navy blue sofa with the plaque hanging over it. The plaque looks to be about two feet wide: blue and yellow embroidered letters that spell out the word FAMILY.

Click, click, click.

I step back for a wider view, capturing a shot that includes the overturned end tables with the dumped-out drawers and a broken ceramic lion.

Snap, snap.

I continue to the window of Julian's room, zooming in on the storybooks sitting on Steven's bed, capturing the bright red and yellow book covers; the top one shows a dancing pig. There are bookmarks sticking out from the pages of the other books—like a well-loved stash of library loot.

I zoom out for the next shot, getting the rest of the room—the broken dresser, the hole in the carpet, a crack in the wall, and a corner of Julian's bed—imagining sleeping here. Steven's obviously been gone for years, but I wonder if his ghost still lingers.

I move around to the rear of the house, suddenly feeling like I'm being watched. There are houses surrounding the yard on all sides. The curtains shift in the first floor window of the apartment building directly beyond Julian's fence. Meanwhile, a police siren blares, and my whole body trembles. I take a deep breath, telling myself that I haven't done anything wrong (aside from trespassing, maybe). Still, I need to be quick.

Like the front, the backyard is overgrown with weeds. A metal shed sits in the center of the lot with its doors splayed open, facing me. There's also a large sandy area with an uneven rock border. I wonder what the space was used for. A grill? An old patio or sandbox?

I edge closer for a better look, but then come to a sudden halt.

Julian's here.

The breath in my lungs stops.

He's crouched beneath a picnic table with his back toward me.

My gut reaction is excitement to see him. But then my brain kicks in and confusion takes over. What is he doing? Why is he here?

The table is tucked in the corner of the lot, behind the shed. The benches have been pulled away. There's a shovel in Julian's hand and a wide gaping hole in the ground.

I take a photo of the mound of dirt beside him.

The shutter clicks.

He looks back at me.

I stare at him through the lens of my camera, desperate to see things clearly, angling close on his face. It's covered in stubble. His lower lip trembles.

But still I'm just as confused.

Julian crawls out from the table. He stands, dressed in the clothes I first saw him in—the hooded sweatshirt, the dark gray pants. He looks like he did that day, at the convenience store, with his cowered posture, when I asked him if he was okay.

"What are you doing here?" I look beyond him at the table. It's big, at least eight feet long and four feet wide. There's a collection of items by the mound of dirt.

And that's when the answer clicks.

I move closer for a better look and scoot down beside the hole. He's been digging up what was buried: a bracelet, a child's shoe, a wedding band, and some old pill bottles.

They're all caked with dirt.

I zoom in close on the ring, imagining it on Mrs. Roman's finger, wondering when she buried it. Five months ago? A couple of years after Steven's death? Did her husband notice when it went missing?

Did he notice the missing shoe? It's a brown lace-up bootie, about the size of my hand, and with a bright red rubber sole.

"Is that Steven's?" I ask.

Julian nods, following my gaze. He comes and sits beside me on the ground. "I was probably seven or eight when I buried it."

"And the bracelet?"

"It was a wedding present to my mom from my father. She obviously didn't want to be married anymore."

"Looks like she didn't want to be taking pills, either." I point my camera lens at the collection of items. Julian doesn't comment, and so I take a couple of snapshots, trying to capture the sparkle of the amber beads through the layers of dirt. They must've been beautiful once.

I peek down into the hole, curious to know what else might be buried, able to see something down there, sitting at the bottom. "What's that?" I ask him.

Julian doesn't answer. He's turned away. His knees are tucked against his chest.

I reach into my pocket for my phone, click on the flashlight app, and aim it into the hole. "It looks like an underground steel pipe." My mind zooms to Peter Hayden. Is it possible that there's a connection? Does Julian know something key?

"What is it?" I insist, pointing the flashlight in deeper. The rod has an iron base with carvings of some sort. Rosettes, swirling vines? The object has a long slender neck and a dish-like platform at the top.

I flash back to years ago, as a kid, digging up old silverware in our yard. Dad said that before there were banks, people used to bury their treasures on their property.

"Julian?"

"What do *you* think it is?"

"I don't know." I peer back into the hole, and then reach in to grab it.

But Julian stops me before I can, grabbing my arm, yanking me back. My phone slips from my grip and falls into the hole, about three feet down.

"What is it?" I insist.

"Do you really want to know?"

I nod. My heart pounds.

Julian pulls on some gardening gloves, repositions on his knees, and lifts the object out. It's an iron candleholder, about fourteen inches long. There's a round crevice at the top for the candle's base.

"Did your mom bury that?"

"No." He shakes his head. His eyes lock on mine. "I did."

My mind reels, imagining what kind of symbolism it held. Did his father used to burn candles in Steven's memory? Was Julian forced to sit still until the candle burned out?

There's a smear of something on the platform top.

Dark red.

Like dried blood.

I look back at Julian's stark white face. "Is this...? I mean, it can't be."

The murder weapon.

"It was an accident," he says; his voice breaks over the words.

The light behind my eyes goes dim. The ground tilts. The world around me whirs. How can this possibly be? And what about Peter Hayden? It was supposed to be him. This was supposed to get fixed.

"My father and I were fighting," Julian continues.

But I almost don't want to hear the words.

"I'd just come home from mowing the neighbor's lawn," he says. "My father was already drunk. And my mother was dead. She was lying in the bathtub, having taken all her pills. Dad said that it was my fault. He came at me, blaming me, calling me a no-good son of a bitch."

I clasp over my mouth. Every inch of me feels like it's racing—like a motor's been clicked on inside my heart, revving up my nerves, rattling every bone.

"He swung at my head with his beer can–holding hand. I swiped it away; the can went flying. It didn't end there. He came at me again, pinning me against the wall by driving his fingers into my throat. I fought back, wrapping my hands around his neck."

"Julian," I whisper. Tears slide over my lips. I can taste the salt inside my mouth.

"His fingers eased from my neck," he continues. "His mouth arched open, and he let out a sputter. But I couldn't do it— couldn't stand to see him in pain. I let go and turned away. But then he came at me again. I grabbed the only thing within reach. Before I knew it, everything went quiet. He wasn't breathing. I went into a panic. I left the house and drove around. When I got back, I buried the evidence, called the police..."

"And gave them the whole beach story."

He nods. "It just seemed easier to say I was at the beach all day. I even went to the beach the following day, so desperate to make the story true. The police seemed to believe me. Everything was going fine on the outside, but I couldn't sleep. I wasn't eating. I just kept looking over my shoulder, convinced I was being watched. They did an autopsy and found the prints around my dad's neck."

"Did they know they were yours?"

"No, and still everybody seemed to assume that my parents were the victims of their own murder-suicide. But then the UPS guy came forward. He told the police about the fight with my dad. Everything turned upside down after that. My only hope was that they hadn't found the murder weapon. But then they got my prints."

"So that's why you came here, isn't it?" I ask, thinking aloud. "Not to dig up the past, but to get the murder weapon, to hide it someplace more secure. It's why you've stuck around so long."

"It's not the only reason." His body twitches. "Your friendship's meant everything to me. I mean, meeting you, it's almost made things worse. As if things could've gotten any worse. Not only have I lost my parents, but I'll also be losing you."

I reach out to take his hand—to pull off his glove and weave my fingers through his—able to feel his body shake. "You don't have to lose me."

"I don't want to lie to you anymore."

I wipe my eyes. "No more lies."

"So, what do we do?" His eyes are red. His face looks pale.

I picture him and his brother in the backseat of his mother's car just minutes before it crashed. "We deal with things once and for all." Still holding his hand, I reach back into the hole for my phone. I click it on.

"Day. *No.*"

"Yes," I say, giving his hand a squeeze. "You're no longer on your own, remember? Trust me."

I can tell he wants to—can see it in his hesitation. His lip quivers. His chin shakes. But still he doesn't utter another word.

And so I press my mother's number. "There's someone I want you to meet."

Monday, October 26

This is my last journal entry in this notebook—not because the pages are all filled, but because I'm giving it to Day. It's all dug up here. There's nothing left to bury.

forty-nine

forty-nine

ONE MONTH LATER

When I get home from school, Mom is already here. She's in the kitchen. I can hear the clanking of dishes. I drop my bag and head in to join her.

"Hey," she says, looking up from a saucepan. There's a wide smile across her glowing face.

I glance over at the table. The crystal glasses are out. The napkins are folded into origami-like swans. "What's the special occasion?"

"I won Pandora's case," she bursts out. "She was released from prison two hours ago."

"You're kidding."

"Not kidding." Mom does a little cheer thing with her balled-up fists, punching the air and shimmying her hips.

"Congratulations!" I smile at her excitement; she hasn't seemed this happy in months.

"So, we're celebrating. I've made fried ravioli. Dad's coming to dinner, too."

He's been coming for dinner at least once a week, including last Friday night, when we ordered all of our favorite Thai dishes, just like old times (and when Dad ate his meal with a fork).

Will the two of them get back together? The vote is still out on that one. But it almost doesn't even matter. They're getting along. *We're* getting along. And I'm spending time with both of them.

After dinner, in my room, I pull Julian's journal from my backpack. It's filled with entries about his childhood, as well as about his time spent on the run. I run my fingers over the cover, thinking how differently his life could've ended up had the car accident never happened, had his father come home on time that day, or had his parents reacted differently to Steven's death.

I've added photos of Julian to my project: a snapshot from

the train depot; pictures of him in the backyard, washing with the hose; and then a photo I snuck at the beach on our date, when he couldn't have looked more beautiful.

"Are you ready?" Mom calls me.

I'm not really sure. I haven't seen Julian since the night he turned himself in, the same night he dug the hole, and I have no idea what to expect.

"Visiting hours are at seven," she continues, "but we have to get there early to register."

Mom's read Julian's journal too. As soon as she heard his confession to the crime, she insisted on taking the case.

I grab the photo album I put together. It's filled with images I thought Julian would like: shots of the ocean at sunrise and sunset, pictures of the moon shining down over Zigmont Beach, and photos of forget-me-not flowers.

I go downstairs and hug Dad good-bye, promising to stop by his apartment tomorrow to fill him in.

"Nervous?" Mom asks, as we climb into her car.

"Nervous, anxious, excited, scared. I don't know what I'll say to him." All I know is that Julian needs friendship and trust the most right now, and so that's what I intend to give him.

"No matter what happens with his case, I know he feels grateful to you."

I feel the same. "I learned so much by helping him."

"Well, then maybe you should tell him that."

•

Julian's not being kept at the Fairmount County Juvenile Detention Facility like before. He's been moved to the detention center in Chesterville, known for its high security, a little over an hour away.

We enter the facility through a set of iron gates. A tall brick wall topped with barbed wiring surrounds the entire place. I gaze out at the grounds. There's a grassy field and a basketball court, as well as a track for running and an outdoor patio space.

Mom parks the car. It looks crowded here tonight. There's a long line for security, but Mom gets us through it pretty quickly by flashing her bar card.

"Are you ready?" she asks, leading me into one of the visiting booths.

I sit down beside her and look toward the long glass window, itching my palms, taking deep breaths, and waiting for Julian to finally arrive.

He appears a few moments later, dressed in an olive-green suit. His skin is smooth. His hair's been cut. The scar beneath his eye has finally healed.

He smiles when he sees me.

I smile too. "I'm ready."

THE END

acknowledgments

I would first like to thank my brilliant and amazingly talented editor, Tracey Keevan, for her invaluable feedback, critical suggestions, and attention to detail. This book is so much stronger because of her. A big thank-you also goes out to Ricardo Mejías for his careful read, and for knowing all the right questions to ask.

Thanks to my agent, Kathryn Green, for her literary guidance and advice. Twelve books together later, I'm enormously grateful for all she does.

Thanks to friends and family members, who are a constant source of support and encouragement. Thank you for reading my work, coming to my events, bringing me coffee (tall, black, no sugar, with a sprinkle of cinnamon), and keeping me inspired. I am truly blessed to have you all in my life.

And lastly, a very special thank-you goes to my readers, who continue to support me and cheer me on. Thank you for reading my books, attending my workshops, coming to my events, entering my contests, sending me your letters and artwork, making book-inspired videos and playlists, choosing my work for your school projects and reports, etc., etc., etc. I'm so truly grateful. You guys are the absolute best.

Also by

LAURIE FARIA STOLARZ